Seducing the Hawthornes

A TABOO REVERSE HAREM

CANDY QUINN

PATHFORGERS PUBLISHING

Preface

Sign up to my newsletter to receive free,
exclusive stories:
http://candyquinn.com/newsletter

*Book Themes: Reverse harem/why choose
romance with multiple men, breeding, teasing, oral, adoptive father,
adoptive brother, adoptive uncle*
Word Count: 50,099

One

I love my family.

Perhaps a little too much according to most.

Sure, I was adopted, but still, they're my family. And so I get the impression most people would not be impressed with me being in bed with my brother, feeling him pound up against my ass as his cock thrust deeply into my pussy.

My brother, Victor, was always the closest with me. And along the way, as hormones hit, and we became adults... things just sorta... happened. A lot.

"Ohhh Priscilla," he moaned behind me, his big hands gripping my hips as I felt his cock throb and pulsate, stretching my tight little hole open. "Fuck, you feel so good," he said, squeezing my ass cheek, giving it a playful slap.

Of course, think ill of me all you like, but know that in a family as rich as the Hawthorne's, your own rules apply anyhow. Inside the walls of the massive, opulent Hawthorne estate, it's the family's rules that matter, and nobody else's.

And it's not like they explicitly had a rule about me not getting rawed by my brothers.

I clutched the bed sheets, my ass pushed into the air as I took him in as deep as I could. My auburn hair was in my face, getting into my mouth as I panted for breath, and with each thrust, my tits bounced, my nipples brushing against the comforter.

"Fuck, just like that," I moaned, feeling him hit that tender spot within me.

The room we were rutting in was an old, opulent bedroom, with a four poster canopy bed, and not a single piece of furniture younger than the Queen of England. Some people might find that stuffy, but there was just something so extra hot about having my brother Victor pounding me amid all that beauty and antiquity.

"Mmm fuck, Priscilla... you're the hottest lil' sister around," he growled, sliding a hand up in under me, to grope and fondle my breast. "I'm gonna blow soon," he grunted, his dick twitching. And this meant it was about time for him to pull out. Almost.

It was always harder to find the words to remind him, especially around certain times of the month. It was like... I didn't want it to end, but also, maybe I liked playing with fire. I'm sure that's what dad would say. Probably not about this, but other things. I was a risk taker.

And there's not really a bigger risk than letting my hot as hell brother cum in me.

My pussy clamps around him as I get closer to my own orgasm.

"Don't pull out 'til I say, I'm almost there," I command, though it comes out as more of a sensual purr.

Victor was an adonis. I could see him in one of the giant antique mirrors right in front of me. He was pale, but his body was sculpted to perfection, the finest of my brothers by far. And like me, he was a bit of a bad child of the family. He even had some tattoos on his rippling, muscular body, that made it all the more enjoyable to watch him pound into me from behind, his big hand grasping my breast.

"Mmmm fuck Priss... you better hurry then," he taunted me, a gleam in his eyes, but it wasn't hard to see he wasn't playing around. He was racked with pleasure and was just trying to play tough as he could barely hold back. He gave my ass a slap, as my little pussy was about to drain him dry.

But I was just so close, and I was greedy for it. The pressure wasn't helping. Or maybe there was something darker at play in my mind. Didn't matter. The bed sheets were twisted around me, balled up into my hand as I pushed myself up, felt his thick, hard cock strike against my inner depths.

"Oh god, Victor, right there, don't stop!"

"I'm not... gonna... stop!" he grunted out, as I watched his pecs bulge, his abs ripple in the mirror. That glorious hunk of a brother staring down at me, eying me for all I was worth, like I was the hottest stripper in the land and he paid just to stare.

But even in that moment, he lost his ability to hold back. Or just gave up trying. Because as he kept pounding into me, he threw back his head and let loose a loud moan, and I felt it... that thick, rigid cock of his erupted. And my brother's rich, virile seed began to shoot out, filling my raw, unprotected depths.

And as risky, dangerous and wild as it was, he kept his promise. He didn't stop.

I lost it.

I'd never felt an orgasm like the one that ripped through me in that moment. The bed was quaking, my screams were echoing off the antiques, and my pussy was milking him dry. We'd never lost control like that, but the way it was rocketing through me, I knew we opened a pandora's box that could never be closed again.

My tanned hips writhed against him, my toned legs helping him thrust into my depths as I moaned like a whore.

And gorgeous, hunky Victor grasped me tightly, held onto me like I would sink and drown in the mattress if he didn't cling to me. And the two of us came so hard, his dick flooding my depths as his glistening body was on display in the mirror.

Not that I could keep watching him too closely, with how fireworks went off behind my eyelids and I was screaming and moaning. It's lucky the Hawthorne estate was so massive, because in any normal house everyone inside it would've heard us, clear as day.

Instead, we got to rut in peace, my brother's seed flooding my fertile depths as he kept his cock planted nice and deep inside me, showing no intention of pulling out or trying to lessen the risk at that point. He just trembled and moaned as he emptied his balls into me entirely, panting out my name.

"Priscilla... oh Priss," he grunted.

"Fuck," I moaned, my head still foggy, my body trembling with the remnants of my orgasm. "We fucked up, big brother." I giggled, raising my grey eyes to the mirror, my dark hair still covering most of my face.

Victor grinned with glee, no sign of having fucked up on his handsome, chiseled face. Certainly not as he stunningly pushed back his own black hair, trimmed short on the sides, but long in the middle and usually swept to the side. But this time he pushed it straight back as he laid lodged deep within me, his cock still throbbing a bit as it spurt it's last.

"Mmm, maybe not, sis... if you'll hear me out," he said, licking his full lips.

I laughed again, wiggling my ass against his hips.

"Yea, you and your cum are still lodged inside me. I'm sure if we ask dad, fuck ups will the kindest thing he says about us," I teased, gathering my own dark hair and pushing it out of my face. "Fuck, it was good though."

He grinned at me, giving me a little nudge forward on the tip of his cock just to tease me. His dark eyes flashing with some mischief of his own.

"No see," he began, as he bent over me, wrapping his arms around me, kissing my spine as he made his way up towards my own dark hair, so like his own. "Grandfather is getting older. And he's still the one who technically owns everything, not father," he said, kissing me repeatedly, tenderly. He was definitely the kindest, softest family member towards me, and I'd always relied on him within the Hawthorne estate. "Who knows how much is gonna filter down to the grandkids, right? Especially the beautiful but adopted granddaughter," he remarked, not exactly making it one hundred percent clear where he was going with this.

It was hard to think with his cock still trapping his cum deep inside me.

"What, so I should get pregnant, marry my brother, and hope that daddy dearest doesn't disinherit you?"

Victor only grinned at my response, seeming terribly amused by it. But he looked into my eyes through that opulent mirror as he shook his head slowly. He reached up, taking my hair with one of his big, strong hands, pulling it back from my face.

"As much as I'd like that, if it could work, we both know it won't," he said, leaning in, inhaling my scent from my hair, then kissing the crown of my head. "You should seduce the ones who matter... like dad, or the favoured son, Malcolm. Uncle Arthur. Or maybe even grandfather himself," he said it all so casually, as if it were such an easy thing.

So I just laughed.

He had to be joking.

Sure, I'd fallen into bed with my favourite brother, but I was a virgin before that. I wasn't exactly eager to slut it up, especially not making it a family affair.

But Victor wasn't laughing, and that gave me pause.

"Oh my God, Victor, you have the worst after sex conversation ever right now," I said with a pout.

He chuckled at that, then guided my head to the silk, leaving it at a tilt as he kissed my cheek, my neck. And his voice grew lower, huskier, as he lay atop me.

"Think about it... if you could seduce one or... several of them, you'd end up coming into a good chunk of this estate. And combined with whatever I get, we would be the new heads of the family. We could do whatever we want here," he whispered so seductively into my ear. "We could openly live as husband and wife, and nobody could say a word to us. Because we'd hold the purse strings... and all you have to do, is seduce them. Bed them. Make them think it was them that knocked you up," he remarked with a hint of a grin forming on his face.

A shiver went down my spine, and I had no idea whether it was excitement or fear. It felt like both.

"Victor..." I murmured, staring at him from the corner of my eyes. "What if one of them actually does knock me up? Firstly. I mean... we did only mess up the one time," I asked, my pussy squeezing his still throbbing cock.

"I can easily make it more than one time," he said with a grin, before biting my ear playfully, tugging the lobe as his still turgid cock gave a singular throb inside me. "But c'mon sis," he said, letting the lobe snap back. "Think about it... do you want to be on the bottom of the totem in this family forever? And hell. Even if I can't be the one who knocks you up, and one of them is legitimately the father... it won't change my feelings towards you. I'm just trying to look out for us both," he said, kissing me affectionately up the neck to my cheek again.

He was so warm, so tender. I didn't really understand what brought this plan to his mind, but it hardly seemed to matter. I just wanted to make him happy. That was how he got me into bed in the first place. Well, it started out playful, and by the time I felt his hard cock throbbing through his pants, it was hard to refuse. Impossible, really.

Just like it was impossible to refuse him then.

"Victor, you really are the bad apple. Which I guess makes me Eve, begging for your seed."

He grinned at that, then wrapped me up in his strong arms, squeezing me.

"Does that mean you'll do it?" he asked, a fire in his eyes. "Because if so, in the meantime... that means I can keep blowing my load in you without holding anything back. And I fucking **love** that idea, sis," he said, rolling his hips and giving me another pump of his cock and a light slap of my ass.

"How much do you love it?" I asked, biting down on my lower lip as I looked back at him. "You kind of have me wrapped around your little finger right now, you pervert."

"Enough to go again... right now," he said with that devious grin on his pale, handsome face. And true to his word, he began to roll his hips, pumping his thick cock into my already cum-filled pussy with a grunt, a moan.

"It'd be worth sharing you with those fuckheads, just to see you as the Lady of Hawthorne Manor," he rumbled, squeezing my breast in his hand as he made my ass cheeks ripple and quake again.

"God... I know this is really fucking wrong, but I want you so bad," I confessed, leaning my head onto the silk sheets, letting my auburn hair shift back onto my face. The prospect of being his cum dump had warped my mind, because I really was considering it. Not because I wanted to seduce them, but because I wanted Victor to be proud of me.

I really would do anything he said. And I'd like it.

Victor and I hadn't left that room for the rest of the day. He'd made me cum and scream my brains out repeatedly, and in the end, I was on board. I agreed to his little scheme. I mean... I had to, right? The risk that he'd already gotten me knocked up was so high, and if I showed up impregnated by the black sheep of the family, we'd both end up with nothing. So time was really not on my side now if I planned to dawdle or hold back.

I wasn't super on board with seducing grandfather, though. He was old enough that the sight of my perky, young tits would likely give him a heart attack before he updated his will. And Malcolm was... intense. Uncle Arthur was on vacation for the rest of the week.

That left dad.

I stayed up all night trying to figure out how to seduce my daddy. It wasn't the easiest thing in the world to have to plan. He could be disgusted. That was a pretty high likelihood. And if I came on to him, he might see it as a transparent ploy to get some cash.

So I decided that it had to be *his* idea.

I just had to plant the seeds.

The next day, I knew he had a business meeting. He was having some investors over, and so the staff would be bustling around for that. And they'd be meeting in the big conference room on the main floor, just across from the pool house.

Just before the meeting was set to begin, I put my plan in action. I got out my skankiest red bikini, the one that barely covered my pink nipples, and went so low between my legs that it only covered half my slit, and decided to go for a swim.

By the time the meeting was in full swing, I was throwing my head back, letting my long hair arc through the air as I slowly climbed out of the pool, my tanned, teen body glistening right in front of the wall length window. I pretended not to see anyone -- it was so bright outside! -- as I turned around, pulling the red g-string from between my shapely ass.

Then, I untied my bikini top, tossing it aside before I dove back into the water.

And of course, for every moment of my little show, I had the rapt attention of the board meeting, and its head--my daddy. I wasn't there for it, but Victor sat in that day, and he told me all about it afterwards.

The way every man in that room--and of course, they were all men--had stared. And even though they tried not to, knowing that I was the board president's daughter, they kept giving me looks whenever they thought he wasn't aware.

But what was most intriguing and important, was that Victor said... daddy's eyes kept going back to me too. Even after he chastised the board to stay focused, growling at them in his authoritative way.

"If you cannot find it in yourselves to restrain your gaze from my daughter's body, then I cannot possibly see how you have the will to run this company with me," he roared at them. But even still, Victor said his eyes kept straying back to me.

That was probably when Sally, our maid, came out to me.

"Miss Priscilla!"

I swam to the edge of the pool, looking up at her with clear, innocent eyes.

"Yea, Sally?"

"Your father is in a board meeting, and asks if you could do your laps in the indoor pool today."

I frowned.

"But it's so nice and warm out. Can't they just shut the curtains?" I asked, excitement building in me. I'd definitely gotten his attention!

"You know your father doesn't like closed doors or

closed curtains. Come now. You can go back out here when they finish up."

I sighed, climbing up the pool ladder, unapologetically topless as I walked the length of the pool. It was massive, and with each step, my tits bounced as I made my way to my discarded bikini top.

"I was going to sunbathe," I said to Sally, who was chasing me with a towel, trying to get it around my shoulders, but I remained just out of reach. By the time I reached my red bikini and slowly bent over to pick it up, I was wet between my thighs, my g-string slowly becoming soaked up between my pussy lips.

My eyes raised to the window, to all the faces within, as I grabbed my bikini top, stuck out my tongue, and stomped off inside in a huff.

Victor said: "If only you could've seen the look on those faces in that room."

Because nary an eye was anywhere but on me, and even daddy, who was prepared to tell them all off, stood staring, his mouth open, ready to deliver his rebuke. But nothing came out. He just watched me move about topless, then head off.

Victor said it took several minutes after I'd gone for anyone to muster up a single word, I'd so affected them all. Of course, what really mattered was one man. And he was almost dead silent the entire meeting thereafter.

Two

It was later that evening, that daddy cornered me. Or rather, had the maid come get me, and bring me to his office. A massive, opulent room, lined with books older than anyone alive, and a heavy, hardwood desk that probably cost more than most houses.

"Shut the door and leave us," he commanded the maid as he stood there in his trim suit. He was a tall, severe man, with gray hair, and a short beard to match it. And his dark eyes were upon me so intensely, I swear I could feel his gaze.

"What in the hell was going through your head today, young lady?" he demanded of me, his voice growly and angry, but... I could detect it. The conflict in his voice. And besides, Victor had told me in between of what happened at the meeting.

I was wearing something more acceptable that night. A long, black pencil skirt and a white blouse. But I didn't wear a bra beneath it, and it was pretty thin and transparent. And I did 'accidentally' pop open a button right between my breasts on the way to his office. Black fuck-me pumps and some matching thigh highs completed the ensemble, with my hair gathered up in an elegant ponytail.

"What do you mean, daddy? I had lots of thoughts today."

He glared at me, but I could tell his anger was thin. Weak. It would burn out in time. And he rounded about the table, coming closer to me, so that I could smell his cologne.

"Flashing yourself like some... harlot! I do not recall hiring my own daughter as a stripper for the board's entertainment today," he fumed, but even then, in his little prepared tirade, his gaze kept dipping down to my chest when it shouldn't have.

"I certainly wasn't paid for the show. It probably put them in a better mood, anyways, so you're welcome. It's not like I knew you'd be in there, daddy. I just wanted to get some sun. You're always telling me I should get outside more," I said as I stepped closer to him, my hand lightly going to his chest. "Besides, it's not like I showed off everything," I said, as if that tiny strip of fabric that had been hiding half my pussy was enough to argue chastity.

His eyes went wide down at me, and I could see the anger in him mingling with something else.

"You very nearly did! Are you aware I could even see your little pink... slit in that bathing suit? Or near abouts!" he chastised me, reaching out with his firm hands to grasp my shoulders. "You really shouldn't wear that when anyone else can see. Even if you keep the top on!" he fumed as his pants strained a little from a growing bulge. "Maybe just... wear it when you're alone, or it's just... us. I don't want your brothers getting ideas either," he said, licking his lips.

My shoulders softened, and I lost a bit of my attitude. I scanned his face, my brows furrowing slightly as I considered his words.

"What do you mean?" I asked, my voice all sweetness.

And I saw it there, the first hard proof my plan was working. His anger--usually so omni-present and impossible to quench by most--melted away, as he gave me a half smile.

"I don't want to stifle your freedom, my dear," he said to me, rubbing my arms and shoulders in his strong, firm grasp. "But... your brothers are men. And prone to desires they shouldn't have. Especially against one as lovely as you," he explained softly. "So... in the future, if you would like to bathe in that suit, or catch some sun... how about you do so in my private pool, on the roof, hm? You can do so there, as often as you like. Any time you like. I'll give you a key to the room, so you can come in whenever you like. As long as you don't mind sharing the space with me now and then," he added with an amiable chuckle.

My clear, grey eyes lit up at the prospect. He'd never offered me *anything* like this before. It wasn't really his idea to adopt me, and he was always cold and standoffish at best. Malcolm really was the chosen child, the rest of us were just disappointments.

But now, I wasn't disappointing him.

And honestly, it felt good to have his approval for once.

"Really? It's supposed to be real hot tomorrow, so I was hoping to work on my tan."

He smiled at me warmly, and I'd never seen him look at me so affectionately before. His hand came up, and he cupped my cheek, caressing it fondly in a way that was so new to me. Only Victor had ever treated me so sweetly. But this was my daddy, and his older hand felt so firm and yet gentle against my smooth skin.

"I'll have everyone sent away. It'll just be you. And maybe me, if I pull myself away from work," he said with a light chuckle. "But we know how likely that is," he said with a grin. And any other time, I'd have agreed. He was never around after all, always yelling at people, running the company that kept the family so filthy rich. But then... I knew he'd find time to take away from work.

"Awesome. Thank you, daddy," I said, leaning in against him, taking my time before placing a kiss at the place where his cheek met his jawline.

"I hate tanlines, so it'll be so much better in private," I said softly, next to his ear, before returning to my standing position. "I might take a nap for a bit, but if you do come up, let me know."

"Of course," he said, his light grey beard hairs tickling my cheek as he wrapped his arms around me and gave me a hug. Perhaps the first real hug he'd ever given me! "Now run along, like a good little girl," he said, smiling at me as he gave my bum a pat, as if I was still a little child and he was shooing me out of his office.

It was turning out to be easier than I thought!

19

O f course, the next day was indeed hot. And the opulent Hawthorne estate was a great place to deal with that. We had several pools after all, the one off my daddy's suite a more recent addition, atop the grand old manor.

It was private, as private as can be. With just that large, flat space, with private seating, the pool itself, and the large wall of glass windows from daddy's room. The place honestly got used very rarely, since daddy hardly ever stopped working, let alone to do something as frivolous as swimming. I was probably the first person to actually come use the pool in years, if ever!

And when I first arrived, there was no sign of him. But that was to be expected, right? He'd want me to ease into the place, get comfortable before he showed up. If his intent was to come have me, anyhow.

And I was still intent on it having to be his decision.

I stripped out of my skirt and blouse, placing them aside, and leaving me in my white bikini and thong. It was a bit more modest, but I wasn't intending on wearing it for long. I put on some sunscreen -- I was going to be out here a while, and I wanted to tan, not burn -- and started to lay back on one of the chaise lounges. My skin glistened in the rising sun, and I turned onto my back, untying my bikini top and bottoms, dropping them to the side of my lounge chair.

Then, I rolled over, and waited.

A pair of dark glasses was perched on my nose, and a gold anklet was around my ankle, but other than that, I wore nothing. My pussy was shaved, the delicate skin exposed to the sun as I spread my legs slightly so as not to get any strange tanlines.

Plus, I was faced directly at daddy's bedroom window, and I wanted him to see me spread them for him.

My eyes fluttered closed, and I got ready to wait.

This time I didn't have the advantage of Victor watching what was going on inside. But I know now, in retrospect, he must've been watching me for some time. Perhaps he'd been jerking it, his dick in hand as he got a good look at my bare slit. Until finally, his resolve wore down, and he emerged.

His footsteps were soft, quiet, and I almost didn't hear him at all until he was standing over me, in naught but his swimming shorts.

"You should let me rub some sunscreen on you, darling girl. I wouldn't want you to burn," he said with a smile, and though he was a great deal older than me--

more than double my age in fact!--and not as buff as Victor, he still looked good. With a peppering of white and grey hair on his chest, his calves well defined.

My pink lips dropped open in a gasp before I smiled, pulling down my shades.

"Oh my god, daddy, you just slipped in! But you're right, I could use some more oil." I shifted to sit up in the lounge chair, one of my legs hanging to the side of the chaise. "I can't reach my lower back very well."

He was wearing a pair of sunglasses himself, but even still, I could see his gaze dip to my chest as I sat there, nude before him. And he sat down beside me, laying a hand on my bare thigh.

"Good girl," he said, licking his lips as he picked up the bottle with his free hand. "I wouldn't want my favourite girl to burn up, and lose her flawless skin someday," he said, opening up the lotion bottle. I'd already covered myself, and either he didn't know that... or didn't care, he wanted the excuse to get his hands on me. Because he was squirting some onto his hand quite soon, rubbing his hands together to get it warm.

"You've become such a beautiful young woman. A proper Hawthorne Lady," he said, as his hands went for my shoulders, then began to rub that lotion into my back in a rather sensual manner.

I let out a soft giggle.

"Dad, don't tease me," I pouted, my hand reaching up to guide my ponytail away from my shoulders. "We both know I'm not as proper as I should be."

His large hands squeezed and rubbed, making it more like a massage than an application of sunscreen. And he worked down to my lower back, letting his fingers curl around my waist.

"Nonsense. You are so close to being the perfect girl, Priscilla my dear," he said, as his two hands move up and up, his fingers along my side so close to touching my breasts. "Perhaps all you ever needed was a firm, guiding hand to take you the rest of the way, hmm? Someone to..." and he leaned in, inhaling the scent of my hair as his hands worked, "take care of you more deeply."

Now, I love Victor. I wouldn't be doing this at all, if it weren't for him telling me to.

But apparently I also had a lot of unresolved daddy issues, because I was getting really wet, and my nipples were really stiff. His body being so close, his hands skirting my tits, his breath on my ear...

Yea, I was really fucking hot for daddy at that moment.

"A firm hand? Your hands are plenty firm, daddy,"

I said as I leaned back, so that his head was on my shoulder, peering down at my supple tits.

And he gazed down at them, his own hands moving around to my stomach, just beneath my breasts. He caressed my tummy there, letting his fingers wander both a little too high and a little too low at times, skirting my mons, my tits. And he kissed my cheek, my temple.

"The Hawthorne family has been without a matriarch for so long," he said, as I felt his cock stiff and throb behind me, hardening against my backside. And he licked his lips. "It's been so hard... on me. Having no lady by my side anymore. Lacking a female figure to help steer the family," he said, his voice growing deeper, huskier, lust tinging his every word.

I shifted against him, my round ass grinding against his cock, even as I pretended I was just trying to get comfortable.

I didn't want to talk. I was afraid if I said anything, that it would break the spell, or do something that would cause him to rethink all this. But my body pressed in against him, my slender arms wrapping around his as my fingers interlaced with his.

Daddy had dropped all pretense of trying to apply sunscreen to me. He was just caressing my skin, holding me tightly in an embrace, as his dick grew ever harder. And he didn't even do much of a job of holding back a moan at the way my ass ground against his bulge.

Instead, he kissed my shoulder, my slender neck, and made his way toward my ear.

"I can't trust anyone outside this estate... or inside it even. But you... my precious girl," he said, his words husky and firm, "you may be the only person on this planet I can trust. Trust to not take advantage of my kindness. My good will and love," he said, nuzzling against her ear.

I covered up my guilt with another shift of my ass against his growing cock.

"You can trust me, daddy. I won't tell anyone," I lied. But at that point, I really didn't want to scare him off, or have him pull away. I was dripping wet, and I was desperate for cock. It didn't even bother me how wrong this all was. How much older and firmer he was, how he'd raised me, how gloriously hard his dick was against my bare ass.

"Can I?" he asked into my ear, before kissing it softly. He sounded so sincere and lusty, and his dick confirmed the lustiness was truly sincere about that. "What if... what I need you to trust me with... is something... very delicate? Very... private. Something that would have to stay a secret between us," he asked me, and I felt his hips instinctively rock, grinding his dick against me a bit.

He was driving me up the wall with desire, and I couldn't help but respond in kind. I was losing control of the situation, but it was careening in the direction I'd set the car wreck in motion towards, so it didn't matter.

"You can trust me with anything. I promise. What do you need?"

His heavy breathing in my ear was the only sound to fill the silence in that protracted moment. And he then gave my neck a slow, sensual kiss that was anything but fatherly. And his hands strayed scandalously far off course, until his fingers were teasing the underside of my breasts, the cusp of my mound.

"I need you, darling. I need... your feminine touch. I need... to be inside of you. To sate my long pent up needs," he finally said, breaking the silence with his obscene confessional. "I need you to fill the role that's been so long empty..."

My legs spread, my hips arching as my wet pussy sought out his wandering fingers.

"You need me?" I asked, my voice so soft and innocent. "You need me to be..." My words trailed off as his hand wrapped around my perky tit, and I let out a moan. My nipple was so stiff, aching for his touch.

He caressed my perky, supple breast, while his other hand dipped lower. His long fingers sliding over my slit, finding it so embarrassingly wet and glistening. God, what's wrong with me?!

"Mmm... I need you to be my good little girl, Priscilla," he murred into my ear between kisses. "I need you to offer this up to your father," he said, punctuating 'this' with his a finger sliding in between my glistening folds. "God, you want it, don't you? You crave me too, don't you my sweet little girl?" he asked, as his finger was joined by another in my tight folds, and he fingered me there by the poolside.

It was impossible to deny.

I was so damned wet, and my hips were lifting, begging for his fingers to slide deep inside me as I leaned back against his chest.

"Oh my god, daddy, that feels so good. Why does this feel so good?"

He kissed me, repeatedly, sensually. Up and down my neck, along my cheek, tilting my head so he could lay a kiss upon my pouty lips for a brief, exciting moment, all while his two fingers slid in and out of my tight little cunny.

"Because this is what you were destined for, sweet child," he husked to me as his dick ached and throbbed for release from his swimwear. "Perhaps your mother always knew. And she wished to adopt you so that when she was gone, I would have the most perfect replacement in her stead... someone so sweet and loyal. So... beyond beautiful," he husked. "Beyond sexy..."

I felt filthy, but I was grinding up against him, begging for his kiss on my skin as he fingered me in the midday sun.

"I want you. I want you to teach me," I said, the words sounding so earnest they surprised even me. I really did want him so bad, and my tender, teen body ached for him. Knowing how wrong it was only made me hornier. I looked down between my legs, seeing my pink pussy spread around his tanned, masculine fingers and gasped.

I could feel his smile rather than see it, and he rewarded me by squeezing and fondling my breast some more, kissing my neck.

"Will you be a good girl for your father, and get on your hands and knees? Beg me to pop your cherry and claim your little pussy with my cock?" he asked, still under the impression I was a virgin. But then of course, I never left the manor, so unless he presumed one of my brothers took it--which Victor did, to be fair--he'd have no reason to believe otherwise.

But as my head grew fuzzy with those thoughts, his fingers slid from my slit, and he lifted them up, to eye those glistening digits before smearing that honey over my lower lip.

I instinctively opened my mouth to receive his offered gift, my tongue cleaning him of my stickiness. I nodded my head as I looked over my shoulder.

"I'll do anything you want, daddy, as long as you say I should. As long as it makes me your good little girl."

I saw his stern face then, and witnessed the way my teasing, filthy words plagued his countenance. His dick throbbed and he licked his own lips, before suckling some of my remaining honey from his digits.

"Good girl," he husked, as he stood up, getting from behind me to strip off his shorts, letting his thick cock spring out. And I was stunned, right away, not by how large and long it was--though it was both of those things!--but how closely his manhood resembled Victor's.

Like father, like son I guess, right?

I stared in shock, and it passed pretty well for being an innocent virgin, because his eyes lit up at my surprise. I had to tear my gaze away as I shifted onto my hands and knees on the chaise lounge, my ass facing him. It was pretty lucky that everything we owned was well made, because there was no way some plastic thing could have handled the motion without toppling over or collapsing in on itself.

My legs were closed at the knees, my swollen pussy peaking out from between my thighs as I looked over my shoulder at him.

"Like... like this?"

He wrapped his hand around his thick cock, and he gave it a few strokes as he admired my body. His eyes alight with desire as he studied my round ass, let his other hand reach out to caress it, to give it a slap.

"So close to perfect..." he husked, then slid his hand down from my backside, to push between my thighs. "Part these a little more, darling," he said, as he got down onto the chaise lounge with me upon his knees. He then guided his bulging cock head to my slit, and teased that purple crown along it.

I did as he said, and just the touch of his cock on my pussy lips sent a shiver of excitement through me. I was being so bad, so deliciously bad, but I wanted it. I wanted him. I couldn't help myself! I was practically trembling like a bitch in heat, and my arms quaked as I tried to keep myself upright.

"Like that?"

"Exactly like that, princess," he husked as he caressed my side, on up to my breast. Where he fondled that perky tit, letting his long fingers sink into the supple flesh. "Now hold on tightly..." he warned me, half a second before he began to push his cock up into my pussy, stretching that slit open wide as he moaned lewdly behind me.

"Oh God. Yes! Take me," I panted out, my hands grasping the edge of the chaise lounge. "Oh daddy, yes. Make me yours!" The words tumbled out so easily, so recklessly, as my unprotected pussy blossomed around my own father's cock. I looked down between my tits, just so I could see it, and the sight made me shiver with the promise of an orgasm.

"Fuck, I need you my princess," he growled out, as he released the base of his cock, then grasped my waist and hip with that hand. He gripped me by breast and hip, and began to pull back his dick, tugging at my tight insides, before he thrust into me again. He moaned loudly, holding nothing back as he began to pump his raw, hard cock into me. Each time making my ass cheek ripple, our bodies slapping together.

"You're mine, princess," he moaned, as he began to fuck me with a ravenous hunger that he'd long let build up.

I might not have been a virgin, but I was still tight, and I gave him a good squeeze just to be sure of things. If he thought he was my one and only, then he'd have no problem spoiling me rotten when I got pregnant with Victor's child. Or his. I really wasn't paying attention to anything that would help me pick the father at that point. It was just reckless, risky fun that made my body sing with desire.

"All yours! All yours! Take me!" I gasped, my brain foggy, my words desperate pleas.

And our wild, incestuous rut grew nearly out of control then. This stunning, older man that was my father, pounding into me hard and fast, his moans and cries filling the air, my own squeals and pants adding to the cacophony.

He pounded that thick shaft of his into me deeply, filling me up as he claimed me just as I begged. His heavy balls swinging up and smacking against my mons, my clit. And he slapped my ass cheek roughly, leaving an imprint of his hand in red.

"F-Fuck you're so tight!" he grunted, his dick spurting pre-cum into me.

He'd been pent up for a long time, I knew. Hadn't felt the touch of a woman in years.

His seed was going to be powerful, and I wanted it, raw, and deep. Victor had no idea what he'd unleashed within me, and my hips rocked against him, taking my daddy's cock to my very depths.

"I've fantasized about this so many times," I

confessed. I wasn't even sure if it was a lie or not at that point.

But truth or no, it made his dick swell within me, throbbing excitedly. And he gripped me tightly, holding onto me with an iron grasp. And we made the hot, glistening rooftop a noisy place of our moans and screams.

"Good girl," he grunted out, and I could feel his dick was getting close. I knew that feeling from the many times of fucking his son, Victor. Of having to be used to the sensation when he was about to blow his load, so he could pull out in time. But I had no intention of allowing that to happen now. I wouldn't want him to pull out.

"You feel so good, princess... too good," he grunted, as he pounded me from behind, making my tight pussy tingle with such forbidden delights. "I... I can't hold off much longer," he panted.

"Claim me. Make me yours!" I hoped they wouldn't be too out of character for a virgin to say. It wasn't like I could beg him to breed me like a bitch, even if I kind of wanted to. But I couldn't let him catch on to my little play. I had to go the distance. I had to take his seed.

And fuck, I wanted to.

"Fuck... are you on the... the--?" but his words

struggled to come out, as he was trying to be cautious even in that moment. But the last thing I wanted was for him to pull out and ruin everything. And his dick was oh so close, ready to erupt. I could feel it, so tantalizingly close!

"Don't leave me, daddy! I need you," I pleaded. I didn't want to have to lie about being on the pill. Who knew what he'd do if he found out I tricked him. My pussy tightened around his cock and I pushed my hips against him, begging for him to unload inside me.

He gave a long, low groan, as he was helpless against me. That tight clench of my pussy, the begging way I pleaded for his release. He was powerless to stop it then.

"Pr--Princess," he gasped, shuddering all over as he gripped me, his two hands holding me so tightly as he shouted. And then, amid his erratic, wild, rough thrusts, he began to cum inside me. So much pent up, thick seed firing out, filling my depths. That proven, virile seed flooding my fertile womb as he shouted to the sky in bliss.

I still don't fully understand why that sent me over the edge into my own heightened orgasm, but that only helped me in that moment. My pussy was acting of its own accord, milking him of every ounce of cum he had to offer me, and my clit was setting off fireworks throughout my entire body. It was explosive and amazing. I'll never forget the intensity of that moment, or the slow drip of reason that began to eek back into my brain as it receded.

And I worried for a split second, as we both finished screaming out our pleasure shamelessly to the sunlit sky, that once he'd got his load out, he'd have regrets and pull away. But instead, as we were panting, he ran his hands over my body, caressing me with appreciation for my skin, and a hint of possessiveness.

"Oh god, princess..." he husked, kissing my back and shoulder as he bent over me. "You're a perfect replacement for your mother," he huffed. "You should really come up and spend time with me more often... day or night. Even sleep in my bed."

Apparently I had magic pussy.

"Am I your good little girl?" I asked, and the sincerity in my voice made my pussy throb with need, a little tremble of desire going up my spine. I really was desperate for his approval, hungry for it with a burning intensity. Even the thought of sharing his bed was... exciting. I could never do that with Victor. It was always too risky.

"Oh yes... yes you are," he said, his husky, post-orgasm voice so rough and sincere, so passionate still despite getting his long pent up load out. "You are my very good little girl," he said, hugging me, caressing me, kissing me. It was more affection than I had gotten in all my days concentrated into one debauched, fucked up moment.

"Come back tonight," he said, nuzzling into my neck, kissing it. "I'll open a nice bottle of wine. And we can... just enjoy ourselves," he said, making that last part sound so very promising.

But as much as I wanted to -- and I really did want to -- I had to make sure that if I was getting knocked up, there was a chance for everyone to think it was their kid. Still, I nodded my head.

"I'll do my best. I've been trying to get Malcolm how to teach me to sail the yacht, though, and he promised he'd take me tomorrow morning, bright and early."

He groaned with disappointment, and I felt his dick throb in me still. He was the patriarch of the family, more than double my age, but still... that cock craved me like a much younger man's.

"Dammit," he rumbled, still kissing and fondling me, especially my breasts. "At least it's Malcolm and not Victor," he muttered, still sounding sore about the possibility of not getting to rail me again that night. "Let me know if things change," he said, before slowly pulling his cock from me, leaving me pussy stuffed full of his pearly white seed.

"Of course," I said as I turned my head to look at him, my bright eyes sparkling in the sun. "I'd cancel it outright, but I've been begging him for months, and this is the first time he said yes."

That much was all true. And the reason he said yes was because I asked him while wearing my pink rhinestone bikini, and I may have grazed his cock with my thigh as I gave him a warm hug.

He was disappointed, but he still smiled at me, reached out and caressed my chest. He leaned in and gave me lips a soft but passionate, unfatherly kiss.

"And did you say you were on the pill? I'll try to do better pulling out next time, if so," he said, licking his lips.

"Mother told me only whores use the pill," I replied honestly with a soft shrug of my shoulders.

That little shrug made his dark eyes snap right to my tits, to watch as they jiggled. And he licked his lips again as his cock gave a twitch of life at the response.

"Good girl," he said, reaching out to pet my hair. "Don't worry. Whatever happens, Daddy will take care of it all," he promised, leaning in to give my forehead a kiss in a more fatherly fashion, before he stood up.

"Back to work, I guess?" I asked as I began to roll

onto my back, looking up at him as his seed dripped between my thighs.

He grabbed one of the clean, expensive towels that the servants had laid out, using it to wipe down his glistening cock as he smiled. He seemed lighter and happier than I ever recalled him being, even when mother was alive!

"Yes, duty calls. Someone has to manage the business empire that keeps us all living lavishly," he said with a smile to her, before simply dropping the towel where he stood.

"We're so lucky it's you," I smiled, letting my gaze dip down for just a quick, immodest peak. "Well, I hope you have a very successful day today, daddy. You deserve it."

He gave a soft groan and bit his lower lip, as I watched his dick throb again.

"I suddenly love that term on your lips, my good little girl," he said with a smile. "Be careful using it though, or I may neglect all my duties for you," he said with a wry smirk and a wink.

We traded a smouldering look before he sauntered off, back to his room, leaving me alone on his private roof. I didn't want to linger long, though.

I had a brother to report my success to.

Three

![ornament]

Victor was a hard one to find. Well, scratch that. Everyone but father was a hard one to find. The manor was so huge, and daddy was the only one who had anything even approaching a real job to deal with. So he could usually be found in his office... well, one of his offices. He had a few.

But Victor could be most anywhere. I had a good idea that he might be down in the basement though. It was a sprawling network of tunnels and rooms, some of them built centuries ago. Apparently the family was afraid of needing to flee an angry mob back in those times. So the tunnels reached out all across the estate, to the old family crypts, to an escape way by the river. And of course, there was a bowling alley, indoor swimming pool, indoor theatre and more down there.

This place was very extra.

The downside is that I could be spending hours searching for him. But as luck would have it, as I walked through the tunnel between the pool and the theatre, I heard something down the hallway leading towards the family crypts.

I went down there, and I found him. Good old Victor, in one of his favourite hiding spots. He was sat back atop one of the intricately carved stonework statues, a book in hand, a tight shirt clinging to his muscles with the zipper down exposing his chest.

"Hey sis," he said, as he looked up from his book at me with a grin.

"Why are you such a goth nerd?" I asked, looking towards the crypts, then back at him with a triumphant smile on my lips. I'd changed back into my skirt and blouse, though I didn't wear anything underneath. I had to pull on some heels before trekking downstairs, though. I was worried he was in the crypts altogether, and no matter how well made that place was, and how much marble they polished on the floor, I was not going in there with bare feet.

"Being a broody goth gets you the hottest chicks around," he said with a confident smile at me as he slipped a gold leaf bookmark into the paperback, then tucked it behind him. He pushed himself to the edge of the carved stone, letting his legs dangle over. "You're looking positively cocky," he said to me with a wry smile.

"Just remember, a girl likes a little bit of possessiveness, but nary a hint of jealousy," I teased, my hand trailing up his chest. "And I like being called a good girl, now."

I could see the excitement on his face, his dark eyes lighting up as he swept back his long black hair. He pushed off the stonework and stood before me, towering so high as he took hold of my hand daintily.

"You fuckin' did it?!" he asked, sounding both surprised and excited. His other hand coming up, caressing my side, my breast, then my cheek.

"Father is in the bag and excited for more, my love," I said as I got up on tiptoes to kiss him. Even in my heels, I needed a little help, given how friggin' tall he is. "It was a lot easier than I thought it would be."

He was clearly pleased with me, and he let go of my hand to slide his big, strong mitt around to my ass. He fondled it, just as he did with my breast, and leaned down to kiss me back. Passionately. He moaned and pulled back after a moment, his dark eyes twinkling.

"Well... you **are** such a good girl," he said with a grin, pulling me in against him, so I could feel his dick twitch. His eyes darted over me, down to my cleavage, then back up to my face. "I just knew no man with an ounce of straightness in him could resist you. Regardless of your familial status," he said.

"What, does this make you feel better about how much raw fucking we've been doing, brother dearest?" I asked, a teasing lilt to my sweet voice. It was a little cruel, but he liked me a little bit cruel. "Knowing that father would fuck me without an ounce of protection, so if he couldn't resist, how could you?"

His hand on my ass squeezed me tightly, then he gave me a spank before hoisting me up with one arm as if I weighed nothing. My legs hooked over his hips and he kissed me deeply, passionately. And I felt his dick thickening in his tight black trousers as we made out.

"Whatever happens, it's gonna be my child that comes out of you. You hear me?" he said, possessiveness in his voice, a steely determination in his eyes. "I'm gonna claim you as my bride, and that child as my own. Just you wait and see," he declared with such certainty and resolve.

"I hope you have a plan. Daddy doesn't care for me spending time with you," I giggled. My mouth went to his throat, licking him seductively as I rocked my hips towards him, my skirt rolling up over my ass. It gave him a better grip on my flesh, and I could feel myself getting slick already. It didn't take much from Victor to get me going.

He was my first, and so much more.

"Mmm, oh yes… don't you worry," he said with a grin as he used his free hand to undo his belt, working open his trousers. "I've been working on the big shot. The toughest nut to crack," he said, as his hard cock sprang out, rigid and ready. "While you're working on the others… I'm gonna work on grandfather. Sewing seeds against the others. Building you and I up," he said, breathing heavier, the lust audible in his voice.

"You're going to have to lie a lot, then," I purred, biting his earlobe lightly. "You and I are the laziest ones of the family." I kissed his neck, suckling it so that I could leave my mark on him. I didn't want anyone to know about us, of course. They might figure out the plan we've been scheming in the dark places of the estate. But I wanted everyone to know he was claimed.

That he belonged to someone.

He groaned and moaned at my affections, and he slid my skirt further up around my ass, leaving it and my pussy bare. And he wasted no time, pushing me down around his dick, so I could feel his iron shod cock split me open and fill me up again. God, it'd only been like… an hour since daddy had pounded me, but I was ravenous for more.

"Mmmm," he moaned, holding me tightly, as he began to move me up and down his dick in a show of just how strong he was. "Don't worry..." he said, his voice breathy, "I've been laying the groundwork for a while... and while grandfather isn't impressed with my accomplishments... he does enjoy my company," he said as we fucked and conspired at the same time.

It was filthy, and I was addicted. I was a lost cause. Brought into the family to be rehabilitated from the crime of being born poor. I was spoiled and given everything I could have ever wanted, and apparently the thing I wanted was my big brother's hard cock as often as I could get it.

"Fuck, this position is good." I sucked his neck harder, leaving my little love marks on his sensitive skin.

He moaned loudly, his husky, masculine sounds of pleasure filling the catacombs around us. And he kept my body pistoning up and down his shaft, like he was some kind of hunky pro wrestler with enough strength to bench press a bus.

"Mmm, just remember... as you mark me... and carry the family's child," he said, fondling a breast with his other hand, having the luxury of strength to do both at once. "That I had you first... that I love you more than anyone. That I'll always come to claim you in the end," he pledged as his dick swelled within me, pulsating, throbbing, our rutting getting wilder, faster, more unhinged.

I whimpered.

God, how did he make me so crazy?

"You know I love you," I whispered in his ear, my pussy taking him deep as he stabbed up into me. "You know we're meant for each other. I could never be myself with anyone but you."

He groaned and grunted, holding me in his powerful arms, pumping his hips in time with the way he lifted my whole body. The result was that I was getting the deepest, hardest fuck of my life in his arms, and got to enjoy the feeling of his biceps bulging, his forearms thick with veins as they strained to pull it off.

"You can fuck... whoever you want... but in the end, you belong to me, sis," he panted out.

"I know."

And I did. As fun as it was, fucking dad, and as much as it fulfilled a dirty, desperate part of me, I would never have done it if not for Victor. If not for our future.

It was true. We were the laziest of the family. But to earn an inheritance, well... It might be work, but it was pretty fun, and it would be a huge win. I'd never have to lift another finger in my life huge.

"I want you to cum in me again. Make sure you cleanse me."

He had to let go of my breast, to hold onto me, to keep up with his building pace. To maintain that ravenous rut we had going, as he hammered his dick into my tight pink pussy. And he moaned into my ear so deliciously.

"I'm never cumming anywhere else but in your pussy again, sis," he pledged to me there in the dark crypt. "I'm gonna make you a full and proper Hawthorne... mother to the next generation. My bride... and I'm gonna lay claim to your tight little holes forever more, I promise you that," he rumbled as I felt his cock swelling, tensing up, approaching its release.

"I love it when you talk dirty to me," I confessed through panted breaths. He was so good, so skillful, and I was a hard time thinking straight, let alone talking. But it didn't matter. My own orgasm was coming in hot and fast, and soon my arms were wrapped around his neck as I gasped and moaned, my pussy squeezing his cock, begging it to cum in my bare pussy.

And though it took a while longer of that exquisite, hard, fast fucking, I got just what I was begging for. He let loose a loud roar that shook the still family crypt. And he started to shoot off that thick, rich, Hawthorne seed that had twice blessed my fertile depths already that day. And he shook and moaned with such intense pleasure, grasping me tightly as he growled out his words.

"You're mine... **my** good little girl, not his. Remember that when he's fucking you."

I shuddered, clinging to him like a helpless rag doll, my orgasm so sweet and powerful it had knocked every ounce of sense from me. I nodded, my body quivering against his.

"Yes, Victor!"

And I gushed around his hard cock, coated his balls, and made a mess of his pants. Fair play, considering he was the one who risked knocking me up in the first place and putting us on this insanely wild trip to seduce my own family.

But as my world spun and I cried out with toes curling, he pressed my back to the wall, and huffed and panted against me. His lips kissing my neck, suckling my ear.

"Whatever happens... just don't forget me, sis... don't forget our bond. Okay?" he begged me, for once making me feel like the one with all the power in this house.

"I could never," I said as I hugged him, letting him see my own vulnerability. I dropped my guard, just an inch. "I love you. This is for us." My words were sweet as I punctuated it with a kiss on his lips. "I love you."

He kissed me back with no less deep of passion, and he held me tightly.

"Fuck every man in the world, if you want. Just remember our love is more special than all the others," he said in a husk. And it was such a beautiful moment in my spoiled, rich life. But it was brought to an early close, as we heard footsteps echoing through the tunnels.

It didn't mean anyone was near, because sound travelled like crazy down there, but it meant we had to disentangle, and his thick cock had to regrettably slide from my bare pussy.

"You know what you're doing next?" he asked me in a low voice, so it wouldn't travel.

"Tomorrow. Malcolm's taking me sailing. Wish me luck," I said as I cupped his seed in me, trying to tug down my skirt. "You have a kerchief?"

"Uhh," he searched his pockets, then pulled out a silk square of fabric, offering it to me with a smile. "Here," he said, leaning down and kissing me again. "I'll see what I can find about uncle Arthur, to maybe help you out there. But Malcolm is gonna be yours. You'll have him wrapped around your little finger in no time," he said with such a delighted grin.

"You sure? He's always so standoffish with me. Like I'm his annoying little puppy that he didn't want but his parents made him take care of," I said as I cleaned myself up.

Victor gave a shrug of his broad shoulders, as he tucked his hefty dick back inside his trousers, and did them up.

"Yeah, he's always been the worst with you, but... I don't think he ever grew out of that phase where a boy picks on a girl he likes and treats her like crap," he said casually. "I mean, we were both horny teens here for a while. And you were the only girl around that wasn't mother, or an old servant. You tellin' me he wasn't jerking it to thoughts of you? C'mon," he said.

I raised a brow at him.

"Firstly, gross, secondly, don't you guys talk about things like that? He ever mention anything that might give me an in?"

"You're about to seduce and fuck him, don't give me 'gross'," Victor teased, before running a hand back through his hair. "And uh... " he took a moment, thinking about it. "He's a sucker for red bikinis, big hair, and pouty, glossy lips judging by his porn habits. Oh, he's also a dick if he gets what he wants too easily. I'd say you should tease him along a bit. Even after you start, just... prolong, keep him going. Give his dick a little suck, but stop before he gets off. That kinda thing. You'll have him under your thumb for sure then. I watched him with those Ailes sisters. The one who just played it submissive got discarded immediately. The one that made him work for it? Yeah, he was her bitch for a good long while, before she moved on."

"See, this is why I love you," I said with a quick kiss on his lips. "I gotta go. I'll find you tomorrow after dinner. I think dad'll want me to be spending nights with him soon, so let me know if you come up with some decent excuses for me. A rolodex," I teased, pulling my skirt down and fixing up my blouse so I looked half-way decent.

He smiled down at me so adoringly, our little scheme going so smoothly. And he gave me a kiss in return.

"Don't worry. I'll come up with lots of good reasons. Maybe 'grandfather' will assign you some new responsibilities for the family that keep you away most nights," he said with a grin. "You look fucking hot as hell, sis," he remarked, "you'll slay them all."

I gave him another smile before I tossed my auburn hair over my shoulder.

"Duh!" I teased, my grey eyes sparkling.

"I'll see you tomorrow, big brother. Stay out of trouble while I'm gone. Jealousy is a poor look on a man, but you don't want to see it on me!" I knew there was no risk of that. I just wanted to make him laugh. I really did love him.

He chuckled and grabbed up his book, waving to me in a playful little manner.

"Don't worry sis. I may not mind you sleeping around, but I'm more of a one-sister kinda lover," he said with a cheeky grin.

I had a big day ahead of me, and after being fucked raw so many times, I needed a nice, long soak in my bathtub, followed by some quality shut eye.

I went upstairs, picking out my outfit for the next day -- my red little bikini and a casual sarong -- and began running my bath. I knew I could have a servant do it, but it always struck me as a bit weird. I mean, it's just turning a knob, how hard is that?

I got it running at the right temperature, added some rose scented oils and a pink bathbomb, sinking into it and letting all the grime of the day get washed away.

I nearly fell asleep in the tub, honestly, and by the time I was wrapping my silk robe around me, curling into bed, I felt like I was in heaven.

I drifted off with the image of Malcolm's disapproving stare sharply in mind.

Four

Dreaming about it was apparently not enough, because I got to see his disapproving face the next morning too as I showed up on the private dock to board Malcolm's personal little yacht.

"You're all ready to go I hope? Because we're on a schedule," he said. The older brother was always so stern and serious. As if he had a lot to be worried about. He treated everything like a dire mission, even though most of what he did was riding the yacht, playing tennis and strutting around like he was cock of the walk.

But luckily once he untied the boat, he looked to me, and I saw him pause for a split-second, before taking my hand and helping me on board.

Malcolm was in good shape. Sure, not as buff as Victor, but his time yachting and playing tennis helped keep him nice and lean and muscular. And he showed a lot of it off, as he was only wearing sandals, shorts and a polo that day. With his bleach-blonde hair slicked back.

"I've been asking you to take me out on this little date for *how long?* I'm ready for literally anything," I said, dropping my bag at my side. Sure, it mostly had a towel and sunscreen in it, but it also had some first aid stuff. I had one of the servants do me up a little baggie of important stuff. I can run my own tub, but I didn't have a good idea about what kind of scrapes you might get into on a yacht. "Why are we on a schedule?"

Malcolm rolled his eyes as he finished untying the last rope holding the yacht to the pier, then he began to head up to the wheel.

"You and Victor. You never take anything serious-ly," he chastised me flippantly, as he started up the boat, and began to take us out onto the water, heading down the stream and out to sea. And all the while, he made a good effort to teach me all the stuff I'd need to know. What certain levels and dials meant, even showed me the little sonar device he had for tracking fish.

But inside, I was seething. He had a way of just

souring my mood, and I was glad Victor said I should leave him wanting, because the idea of hopping off the boat and leaving him to die of blue balls was so satisfying at that moment.

I did my best to listen, repeating back what he said at appropriate times to show I was paying attention and absorbing all the information. But all the while, I was working up to something. A little brush of my hand against his thighs as I leaned in, taking a moment to readjust my bikini top by running my fingers up along my breast beneath the fabric.

It was fun, and a whole lot better than letting his snotty attitude get me down.

He was a tough one to read, because he always looked so sour and bitchy. But the shiver that went through him at that little brush was a dead giveaway. He was interested in me, even if he really didn't want to admit it.

"Here, we're out far enough now," he said, as the shore was lost in the distance, and it was just us out on the water, with the warm sun beating down upon us. "We can take it easy for a while, do some fishing," he said. But that was certainly not my idea of taking it easy, and it'd be hard to titillate and tease him into making a move while handling slimy fish.

"I didn't know you knew how to take it easy," I

teased, my grey eyes twinkling at him as my fingers went to my sarong, untying it and tossing it aside. "That's not my idea of taking it easy, though," I confessed.

He was half turned away from me when I began talking, but as my sarong dropped, and I was left standing there in just my bikini and sandals, he glanced back. Then did a double-take. I had worn that trusty red bikini again, the one that had snared the board and daddy all at once. And it was impossible not to notice when Malcolm's eyes lingered at the teensy little triangle of fabric that only half covered my pussy. And his mouth dropped open as he was silenced for a moment, unable to do anything but stand there, staring at me, slack-jawed.

"What?" I asked, my brows furrowing. "Oh my god, do I have a bug on me?" I asked as I looked down, my hands roaming over my skin as I twisted about, giving him a good view of my round ass, the red g-string completely lost between my sumptuous cheeks. "Don't just stare, Malcolm, help me get it off!"

"Uh, um yeah," he said, as I'd laid him speechless for so long. He then hesitantly reached out, or rather... confusedly, because he didn't seem too hesitant. And he began to caress my skin in a very weak impersonation of trying to wipe a bug off me. And I felt his hard, work-worn hand slide over my back, across my thick, bubbly round ass.

"Did you get it?" I asked, doing quite good at playing innocent. I just needed him to get hooked, and then I'd be able to reel him in. But I had to make sure the hook was deeply implanted. It wouldn't do for him to break free and avoid my bait in the future.

Get it? Fishing puns.

"Umm, uh, lemme see..." he said, and he copped a few more groping feels of my ass and thighs, before he reluctantly gave up the opportunity to feel me. "T-there, I think it's gone now," he said, rubbing his other hand at the back of his neck, and looking nothing like his usual arrogant, cock-sure self.

"Good. I hate creepy crawlies on me," I said as I walked towards one of the chairs he had on board. "Come on, get some sun with me. I don't need to catch a shark or whatever, but out here, I could get a killer tan."

Normally he'd have rolled his eyes, said some sneering remarks and went about his own business. But instead, this time he followed after me, his head foggy with desire as he stared at my ass.

"Y-yeah. A nice tan would be good for us both. Wouldn't wanna look like Victor," he said with a half laugh. Which, while a jab at the man I loved, was as close as I'd seen Malcolm get to being casual and fun with me.

"There's just one thing," I said, stopping in my tracks, making him bump his hard cock right into my lower back. He and Victor were nearly the same height, and I was definitely a good foot shorter than him.

And I could feel he already had a bit of a chubby in his shorts, and he wasn't as quick to pull it away as he should've been.

"Uh, yeah? What's that, Priss?" he asked, looming over me and desperately trying to rein himself in, get control and act more like his normal self. But he seemed drawn to my scent then, leaning in and inhaling it from my hair a little.

I couldn't remember him ever calling me Priss. Prissy was his go to. His Prissy little sister.

"I really hate tanlines. I think they're tacky and cheap." I turned to look at him over my shoulder, my nose brushing against his, seeing as he was so close. "Is that okay? I mean... we're family and all."

The way his eyes widened at that... I would've laughed, if I wasn't trying to seduce him. Instead I had to keep it to myself as I watched my usually stern, serious brother look utterly floored, until finally he gave a vacant nod as he stared.

"Y-yeah, I mean," he laughed, his eyes going down

to my bikini thong, staring at the little peek of pink it gave. "It's not like... there's a lot of difference between a bikini and nude anyhow, is there?" he said, tonguing the seam of his lower lip as his own shorts began to tent.

I giggled.

"Not when you buy a bikini two sizes too small," I said as I let out a sigh of relief. "I'm so glad. I didn't want to make it weird." My fingers went to the nape of my neck, gathering up my dark hair. "Would you help me out of it? It's always getting tangled up in my hair."

"Y-yeah, sure!" he said, as he shifted, getting behind me and helping undo that string that held my ample tits in place. He was eager to see me out of that suit, even though--as he'd said--it left little to the imagination anyhow.

"No need being shy around each other, right? I mean, we're family. It's all normal, and there's nobody around for miles," he said.

"Plus, aren't we, like, on international waters now? Doesn't that mean nothing's illegal?" I asked, as innocent as I could manage. I didn't earnestly believe that, of course, but... I wanted to plant that seed in his head, so he'd plant his seed in me.

He gave a soft little laugh, "Well actually--" he

began, but then as I turned a bit, the words were stolen from him.

My tits barely moved as they were freed from the bikini top, as perky as they were. I ran my fingers down over them, pushing the bottom bikini string down a little.

He was staring at my breasts, licking his lips as he was transfixed.

"Y-yeah. Anything goes. Anything at all," he said, running a hand back through his hair, almost like he was stressed out for exams again. "So, uh... I hope you don't mind my saying, but... you've really filled out this last while, Priss," he said.

"Right?" I asked, my grey eyes wide as my hands went to my tits again, and I bounced them. "Fuck, finally, right? They're really heavy, too. Wanna feel?"

His eyes widened in surprise at that, but he was rebounding a bit. Or maybe it was just instinct that was making him nod, and his hands reaching out.

"Y-yeah," he began, apparently unable to say that word anymore without fucking it up. It was like my bare body was scrambling the communications between his brain and mouth. "You were a slow bloomer, but..." his hard hands came up, cupping my breasts, lifting them in his palms, caressing them with his thumbs. He was smitten. "Fuck... I'd have sworn father bought you fakes as a present before laying my hands on them," he said, transfixed on my stiffened pink nipples.

II laughed, then smacked his hand away.

"Don't be gross. I'd never get falsies," I said as I turned to the lounge chair, undoing the rest of my bikini top and letting it fall lazily to the ground. "Would you do me a favour and grab me a sparkling water? I'm parched." I settled into the chair, lifting my hips and beginning to push my bikini bottoms down. I got around mid thigh before I stopped.

"Actually, I'll leave these on. I don't want to make things weird."

"N-no! Weird? How would it be weird?" he said, his eyes wide with alarm, as if afraid he'd lose out on that shot to see my pussy utterly bare. "You take it easy, get undressed, while I get you that water. Remember? It's anything goes out here. And nobody ever finds out about it," he said as he reluctantly began to head towards the cabin, to grab that drink.

He was back in a flash, only his shirt was gone, and he was showing off his lean, muscled form, nicely tanned, unlike Victor. But he also had something else with him. A bottle of champagne--the real stuff--and two flutes to pour it into.

"Wow, if I had any idea I was going to get spoiled

like this, I wouldn't have taken no for an answer when I asked you to take me out," I said, leaning back in the lounge chair. My bikini bottoms were stuffed beneath the chair, my legs bent at the knee, one calf pressed into my knee as my sandal dangled off my foot. I knew I was giving him a good shot of my pussy, pink and needy, hidden between the shadow of my thighs.

And he didn't pass up the opportunity. Especially since he'd come back with a bit more of his usual strut in his walk. He was clearly trying to rein himself in, be more his usual cocky self. But the fact he kept the shorts, tells me he was afraid of letting it slip that he was so into what he saw.

"I got you the water, but hey... I thought, why half ass this thing? So I broke into the emergency champagne," he said with a half smile, as he began to pour up the sparkling wine. Though his eyes stared at my puffy little pink pussy, and he accidentally spilled some champagne onto the deck. "Whoa!" he said, trying to laugh it off, as he offered me the tall glass.

"Emergency champagne, huh?" I laughed as it fizzed all over the glass, though I quickly took it all the same. "Here's to always being prepared," I said in a toast, lifting my glass towards him.

It was clear he was wanting to liquor me up, like I was just another girl he was out to seduce. His first step to rebounding off his embarrassing bout of fluster earlier. But he poured up his own glass and raised it.

"Here's to cutting loose, with no rules," he said instead, before clinking his glass to mine.

"Ohhh, I would just love to see you actually cut loose," I said with that shimmer of excitement in my eyes as I looked him up and down. I sipped my champagne, licking the glass free of the remnants that had spilled over it.

"Tell me, Malcolm. Do you have a girlfriend yet?"

He was sipping his champagne, then gave me a shrug of his shoulders.

"Nothing steady right now. But I've not been lonely, if that's what you mean," he said with that cocky, wry smile on his face. "Scored a girl or two recently. Why? Don't tell me you're seeing someone finally," he remarked with a laugh, it was meant to sound like a joke, but I could detect a tiny hint of worry there. He didn't want me to answer 'yes I am'.

"Malcolm, this is my first time off the estate in like... months," I said with a roll of my eyes. "Who am I going to be seeing? Victor?"

Okay, maybe I was doing a little digging about their relationship. I needed to know what he thought of Victor so that he and I could plan this best. But I wasn't going to badmouth him to Malcolm. That would be a betrayal, and I wasn't going to play that game.

Malcolm just laughed at that thought, finding the idea absurd.

"Wouldn't that be fucked up?" he said, drinking some more champagne, then topping off his glass again, and moving to do the same to mine. "Nah. You need a guy who gets out of the basement now and then," he said with a confident grin. "A guy who can take you out for a good time," he began, clearly thinking himself the ideal partner in this scenario. "Y'know, I'm not all business. I've had a lot of party's out here on this yacht, for instance. You don't think I carry booze here for a joke, do you? I know how to have a good time," he said, and he hit a button on a remote beside him as he sat there on the seat across from me, and music began to play out over the deck of the ship.

I turned onto my side, my thighs closing around my wet cunny, my breasts shifting slightly as I looked at him.

"You're all business with me," I said, my gaze dropping to his shorts. "I mean, you won't even get a proper tan with me. It's a bit fucked up that you're letting your sister be nude on your boat by herself."

His eyes lit up at that, and he grinned unevenly.

"Well... I just didn't want to intimidate you, little sis," he said, licking his lips as he stood up, towering there, hooking a thumb into the waist band of his shorts and letting them sink down low, to show some of his adonis belt. "I mean, you've never even had a proper boyfriend. How are you gonna deal with the sight of all this?" he asked, taking another sip of his champagne, and then doing his best to confidently tug his shorts down, letting his half-turgid member dangle exposed as his shorts fell to his ankles, and he stepped out of them.

I sized him up, my gaze slowly raising to his eyes as I smiled.

"Well, I don't have anything to compare it to, so I don't know whether to be intimidated or not," I said as I rolled onto my back, my legs spreading to either side of the lounge chair as I sipped my champagne. I was trying to play it slow. Drag it out. Tease him. Make him hate me a little, so that he'd want my approval all the more.

And I could feel the look he gave me, without even seeing it. That wasn't the reaction he was wanting or expecting. But he rebounded, drank some more champagne, and then stepped out of his sandals.

Truth was, he looked to be about as big as his father and brother, though it was impossible to know without him getting hard all the way. It seemed the family really had a strong resemblance in that area, which was pleasant for me.

"Trust me, you should be," he said, sounding confident in that. "Every girl I take out here ends up screaming from it. 'It's too big,' 'take it slower', 'ease it in'," he recited as he strode to the end of the boat, giving me a brief view of his own tight ass, before he turned and leaned back, his arms stretched across the railing in both directions as he looked to me, the music thumping.

"That sounds painful," I said with a smirk. But oh... I did want to scream for him. But I wouldn't be a mewling pussy about it. My eyes went back to his cock, then his face. "Show me how big it gets. I want to see."

He tried not to show surprise at that, and acted confident, like I was always gonna ask. But he took a moment to drink some more, then looked back to me.

"I know this is your first time seeing one for real, sis, but... they don't just rise up on their own, y'know," he said with a cocky expression. Though damn him, he was hot and handsome. "Maybe do a lil' somethin' to coax him up. Or are you afraid?"

"Ya right, as if anything your little Prissy Sister can do that'd get you excited," I sighed, looking just a teensy bit down about it, as if it disappointed me to be such a failure for him. "Can't you just like... jack it or whatever?"

He was doing a much better job of feigning his usual confidence, and he gave me another shrug. He ran a hand down over his rippling abs, through his trimmed pubic hair, teasing the base of his cock.

"I don't jerk off. Ever," he said, sipping some more champagne as if he was the hottest man on earth. When in reality he was just in the top three or so. "You don't have to when you can score hot women to handle your load for you," he said, sipping more drink then looking back to me from out over the ocean. "You finger yourself a lot?" he asked.

"Oh my god, don't be gross." I drank the rest of my champagne, setting my glass aside. "I'm a lady, not a harlot. But I guess that's why you're half stiff looking at your baby sister's tits. How long's it been since your last nameless conquest?"

He grinned cockily at me, letting his eyes move over my body before shrugging again.

"Been a couple days, sure," he said, and I could tell he was stretching the truth there. "But when you've got a libido like mine, that might as well be an eternity," he said, licking his lips. "But c'mon, sis. You wanna see it full size, help me out here," he insisted. "Remember? Nothing's wrong or illegal out here."

"Oh, wrapping my fingers around your cock would certainly be wrong," I said, my tongue rolling over my full lips, making them glossy. "I'm pretty sure father would disinherit both of us if he found out the first dick I touched was yours."

"Hey," he said, holding up a hand as if in surrender, "I never said you have to touch it. Especially not with your hands," he said, acting faux-offended, but I could see he was beyond being grossed out by the idea of fucking me. "Could always use your mouth," he grinned. "Kiddin'. Just saying... you could maybe touch yourself a bit."

But as confident and in control as he was trying to act, I could tell he was getting antsy to make progress with me.

"Malcolm, I'm pretty sure sucking you off would be worse. Come on," I said, leaning forward, batting my lashes at him. "I'll let you stare at my pussy as you stroke yourself. That's a pretty fair trade, isn't it, big brother?"

And despite all his stern exterior of being cocky, confident and in control, I could see him buckling. He licked his lips, went to drink some more champagne, but... hesitated.

"Fuck, Priss..." he said, rolling his eyes, looking away for just a moment. But his gaze was back on me almost instantly. "Alright, fine," he said, "just to show you what it's like. But don't tell anyone I was jerking it. I've got a reputation to uphold," he said, as he let his hand slide back down, to the edge of his dick, skirting the base of his manhood. But he was clearly waiting for me to give him that nice, good view before he began.

"I won't tell anyone that I was naked on my brother's boat, watching him jerk off as he stared at my pussy," I promised, a smile on my lips. And then I shifted the chair so that it was facing him, my feet going to either side of the cushion as I spread my legs nice and wide for him.

He took in a deep breath then, not able to hide in that moment how relieved he was that I gave in that tiny bit. But at the sight of my pussy, bared right before his eyes, he bit his lower lip and I watched his cock twitch with life instantaneously.

"You're lucky you're so damn hot, Priss," he said, as his long, strong fingers wrapped around his dick, and he began to tease his veiny length a bit. But his gaze never left my pussy and tits, I was his porn for the day, it seemed. "Here... you got what you were after. Watching your brother jerk off in front of you," he said, as he began to pump his length, which had so quickly began to rise up towards its full length, and once more showing that the Hawthorne family were all closely matched below the belt.

"This is the hottest thing I could imagine," I said earnestly. I was quite enjoying the show, and my pussy lips were starting to slicken, whether I liked it or not. "I wish I could take a video, but I wouldn't dare let that get leaked. I'll just have to remember this very, very well. Here, come closer. I want a better look."

Malcolm responded well to that, his cocky look melting a bit as he grinned at my reaction. And he gave a good show of it too, tilting his hips just enough to let me get a nice view of just how long and thick he was, as his hand travelled up and down that length. And that bulbous, purple crown, was throbbing as it leaked pre-cum, leaving it to glisten in the sun.

"Of course, sis," he said, as he pushed from the edge of the boat and came closer. The scent of his musk on the air as he kept pumping his shaft with a smooth, practiced motion that showed he was full of shit when he said he never jerked off before. "How's this?" he asked, as he stood there, right beside my seat, his dick almost at eye level with me as it pulsated eagerly.

"Fuck, that's amazing," I said, letting my own hand trail down, sliding between my thighs. My fingers gathered some of my honey, drawing it out before I pulled my hand away. "Oh my god, Malcolm, what are we doing?"

A flitter of alarm passed over his face, and he crouched down, letting go of his dick. And he reached out to me, with the same hand that had just been on his cock, to brush his fingers along my cheek.

"Hey, it's okay, Priss," he said with a charming, disarming smile, even as his cock bobbed. "I know it feels a little weird... but think about it. You've never gotten to do anything with a man before. It was bound to feel a little weird no matter what," he said, clearly on the offensive of trying to win me over.

"Yea, but... I mean, there's no way that's going to go down on its own, now," I said with a flick of my eyes up to his. "Can... Can I taste it? Just like... a little suckle, nothing serious. Practically just a joke, you know?"

Excitement coursed through him at that offering, and I saw the look in his eyes. He nodded before he was even verbal again, but that wry, confident smile was returning to his face.

"Just a joke, yeah," he said, as he slowly rose back up, and placed his large hand around the shaft of his cock. He gave it a few more strokes for my benefit, making a show of it, the way his heavy balls swayed. And then he presented it right in front of my face.

"Just a little suckle... as an in-joke between us, sis," he said, grinning.

"I can't believe I'm going to do this," I said, as if I just could not resist him. My grey eyes met his as my mouth opened and my tongue peaked out, tasting the head of his shaft. Then I took his full crown in between my lips and began gently sucking, as if it were a lollypop.

The look on his face was exquisite. Because while I knew he was bullshitting about not jerking off, I know he wasn't bullshitting about sleeping with a bunch of girls over the years. He was experienced. And yet... he reacted as if I was the first girl to ever put her lips and tongue to his dick.

"Ohhh fuck, yeah sis," he began, licking his lips as I felt his cock pulsate wildly with desire against my tongue. "Your first taste of cock," he said, giving the shaft of his member a slow stroke, causing some pre to spurt onto my tongue.

Luckily, Victor had gotten me pretty damn use to taking cock, so I knew there wasn't any worry about him cumming just yet. Hawthorne men had stamina, anyways. So I decided to just enjoy, to suck on the head of his cock as if it were the most delicious treat I'd ever been offered.

And then I pulled back, touching my lower lip.

"Oh my god, don't tell anyone I did that."

I could see the pang of disappointment as I stopped, but he managed to play it cool. He smiled down at me, took his hand off his dick and caressed my hair, which I had done nice and well styled, to fit his tastes.

"What happens on the yacht, stays on the yacht, sis," he said, his dick pulsating with need. "So... how did you like it, huh?" he asked.

"It's a lot different than I expected," I said, keeping it ambiguous. I felt like I was constantly just trying to toy with him, to keep him off his game. The second he got too cocky was the second I knew that I'd be just another lay to him. "Could you get me some more champagne?" I asked as I grabbed my empty flute glass.

I could tell he was disappointed with that response, but he responded "Sure" immediately to my request. He bent down, grabbed the bottle, then topped me back up to full. He was not giving up on me, just as Victor predicted.

"You want to hear a confession, sis?" he asked with a smile, as he put the bottle back down, and pulled his seat up closer to me, until it was nearly against mine. And he sat down, legs open wide, so that his thick cock was still right there beside me, exposed.

"Ohh, I always want to hear a confession." I took a

polite sip of my champagne, my legs delicately closed in between his, my knees almost brushing against his sack. "I hope it's a good one, though," I said, taking another sip.

That little brush of a contact made him shiver, despite the heat of the day and the sun on our exposed bodies. But he licked his lips, downed the last of his own champagne before putting the glass down and then leaned forward, elbows on his knees.

"You shouldn't feel too embarrassed, Priss..." he began, his voice hushed, as if someone might pop up out of the water in the middle of the sea to spy on our conversation. "In fact... I used to... jerk off to thoughts of you. Y'know... you were the hottest girl in my life," he said with a confessional grin.

Victor was fucking right.

I didn't even tease him about the fact that he claimed to *never* jerk off. It was kind of flattering. If you're into that sort of thing.

"You did?" I asked sweetly. "Is that why you got so cold to me the past few years?"

He gave a bit of a shrug, his smile more casual and innocent, not his usual cocky one.

"Yeah, you got me," he said. "Didn't wanna let on how much of a hard-on I got for my little sis. I wasn't on international waters at those times, remember?" he said with a playful wink. He was pouring on the charm with me, in more of his usual manner with women, I could tell.

My gaze dropped to his lap again, and I gave it one more soft, longing look.

"I have to head below deck, Malcolm. This is just... a lot, you know?" I said. I didn't want to be just another lay. I wanted him to be desperate for me. Begging me to please, please let him cum in me. That wasn't going to happen if I gave in right here and now, like I wanted to.

And right away, instead of a sign of him backing off or losing interest, I could see... he was getting desperate to assuage my nerves, and keep me there. He reached out to place his hand on my knee, not restraining me in any physical sense, but just trying to compel me to stay.

"Hey I'm sorry," he said, sounding more concerned for me than I'd ever heard him. "I didn't mean to weird you out. Don't go down, please," he begged me, sitting there, "this is the nicest time I've had with you. And... and we don't have to do anything. Lawless international waters or not," he said with a laugh. "I'd just like to make you comfortable and happy out here. Especially after I stupidly put off taking you for a sail for so long. Wasting so much time," he said.

And I could see in his eyes, the growing yearning for me, that was nearly overwhelming him.

"Malcolm... You're so hot, and I really want you to keep being nice to me. And I want to, you know, do more. But it's wrong. Dad would kick me out if he knew." That part was probably true. "I feel so torn. What do you think we should do?"

His gentle but hardened hand caressed my knee and thigh, and he acted so kind, even as his dick throbbed excitedly.

"We're both in the same boat here. I mean," he laughed a little, "literally and figuratively. Father would kill me. So... we're both gonna keep this all a secret, right? No matter what we do next. I mean, I'm never gonna forget the sight and feeling of your lips wrapped around my cock, but... nobody'll ever know. You're not just some conquest, Priss," he said, leaning in until his face was almost to mine. "I love you. As my sister, and... I think... a little more," he said, wetting his lips.

He looked absolutely smitten.

"You mean that?" I asked, my face so near to his. "You really think you... love me? You've been so cold to me, I always just felt like I was annoying you. But now that it's all out, where do we even go from here? Just sail home, pretend this never happened?"

His hand tightened on my thigh at that, sliding up it a bit more. It was like he was clinging to me, so I wouldn't drift away into the sea and be lost to him.

"I mean it," he insisted. "And... and I'm sorry for being so cold to you. I really am. I... that was so stupid of me," he said, wincing a bit at his own antics. "But... I know it wouldn't be simple or easy. At first, but... hear me out," he began, licking his lips, so close to me he nearly licked mine as well. "We can escape out here as often as we like, to be together in whatever way we want. We could do it every day the weather was fine, if we wanted. And... and I know that might sound... not ideal, but," he began, trying to convince me, "in time... I'm likely to inherit a big chunk of the family estate. And then... we can do whatever we want. Live however we like. Out here in the middle of the sea, or... back home in our own mansion," he said with a tinge of excitement.

Beneath the surface, him and Victor were so alike, it was really no wonder they didn't get along.

"And what do you want?" I asked, my grey eyes boring right into his soul as I stared at him so closely. "If this were one of your fantasies, what would I do right now?"

His eyes were wide, locked on mine. And his full lips parted to say something. But nothing came out.

Instead his hand grasped my thigh, and he leaned in, head tilted. And our lips met. He kissed me, lovingly, passionately, but slowly. His tongue sliding into my mouth as he gave me what he assumed was my first real kiss. And one of his hands came up to grasp my breast, fondling it gently.

His machismo had been stripped away, and in its wake, I found a strangely sincere and tender Malcolm. It wasn't what I expected. It was... really nice.

My shoulders relaxed as my mouth opened for him, letting him kiss me, learning his rhythm and method. My breast was a handful for him, my pinkish nipple stiff and excited against his tender touch.

How much of this was who he really was? And what he'd been holding back for me? And how much was like, as Victor predicted, that I played the seduction game perfectly? I couldn't say for sure. But I knew I had tapped into something in Malcolm that had been there for me. And... he was a great kisser. And his hand never got too rough on my breast.

We sat there, making out for a nice long while, and he never sought to push things further in a hasty manner. But finally our lips broke, and he kissed me again, briefly, before speaking in a low, lusty voice.

"I want you so bad, Priss... I want to take you on my boat. Make it ours," he said, kissing me again. "I want to be your first," he professed, sounding so sincere and in love.

It wasn't like I got off on lying to him, seducing him against all his better reason.

But it wasn't like that was a turn off either.

"You said the others were always... screaming out," I said, coquettishly. I didn't want to make this too easy on him, even now. Even when I felt my snare tightening around his neck.

"I'll be real gentle," he promised immediately, missing not a split second of time to reassure me. "I'll take care of you. I'll eat you out first, to get you nice and ready. Then ease it in, and... take it at a nice slow pace for you. I promise. I was just bragging before. I mean... it's true, but sex doesn't have to be rough," he said, caressing my thigh, my breast. "Or... or we could just take it real slow. And stick to using our hands, or mouths. Until you feel comfortable," he said with a smile. "I wouldn't mind coming out here just to watch each other masturbate, honestly."

It was so cute I swear I was going to die right then and there.

"Maybe we..." I began, trailing off in thought. "I mean, I've never had anyone touch me. I don't know what it's like. But isn't it gross to have to, like, eat a woman out? The guys I knew at boarding school were always talking about how disgusting women's bodies are."

His eyes flashed wide, as if in anger.

"No way! That's bullshit!" he said defensively. "And you? I bet you taste like heaven, sis," he said with a smile, looking more sincere than I'd ever seen him. "But... we can just start with me touching you. Here," he said, rearranging the cushions and straddling his lounge seat, "You can rest back against me, and I'll wrap my arms around you. Hold you warmly, and touch you," he offered.

Of course his dick was still rock hard and jutting out, so that'd be jammed into my back if I did it.

But honestly, it sounded like a sweet deal.

"And if I call it off, we go back to this all being an inside joke that we'll never tell anyone else?"

He nodded to me immediately, his eyes shining in the sunlight.

"It'd break my heart, but... yeah. I'll sail you back home, and it'll just be our little memory. Something I hold onto forever, but never share with anyone," he professed, sounding so sweet and sincere as he sat there, waiting for me to come to him.

"Okay, but..." I trailed off as I stood up, moving to

his chair and beginning to get comfortable against him. My tanned ass pressed against his throbbing cock, my long legs bent to let him get better access to my sex. "Don't get me off."

His long, strong arms wrapped around me without delay. And he held me warmly, closely. So much like the many nights that Victor had held me, when I needed comforting, or... we were just being sweet.

And Malcolm kissed my shoulder, then my neck, as his hands caressed my stomach, my thighs. Then they wandered in along my smooth, inner thigh flesh as he spoke to me in my ear softly.

"Why don't you want to get off, sis?" he asked, his voice hushed and quiet, as his fingers trailed gently in towards my sex, and he begin to tease open my labia.

I was embarrassingly wet. Like, soaking wet. Sea-world wet.

"I'm afraid," I confessed. "If you make me cum, it'll open up all these... feelings. And then next week, when I see you sail off with another woman, it'll break my heart. So just... play with me. Let me play make-believe."

His dick was throbbing wildly against me, it reminded me of Victor and I's first times playing around together. And Malcolm held me so gently, caressed me, kissed me, nuzzled against the crook of my neck, while his fingers toyed in the copious honey of my pussy.

"God sis... you're so wet. I've... wow, I just knew you had to want me too. Deep down. And..." he swallowed anxiously, "God I feel like such an idiot." His fingers very expertly began to tease around my clit, parting my folds, edging towards the entrance of my cunny too. "I'd swear off all other women. If it meant... if it meant I could hold you like this more. If... we had any shot at something special and long lasting together," he husked into my ear. "I'll do it, sis. I promise I'll never touch another woman," he said, as his fingers worked my slit with such expertise, only Victor could outperform him.

But to be fair, Victor had a lot more time to learn my body in particular.

I didn't hide my pleasure from him. I didn't hold back on the soft sighs and encouraging moans, and my ass kept rocking against his dick as it throbbed excitedly. I knew it was going to be inside me before we sailed back, and I was thirsting for it, but I had to keep myself in check. Not be too desperate. Not be too easy.

"That feels so good. It's nothing like when I touch myself," I purred. "Your hands are so rough, but... it makes it better."

For his part, he did nothing to hold back his moans

and groans either. And there were a lot, with my thick, bubbly ass grinding on his hard, needy cock. But he never lost focus, fingering me with such dedication. It felt so nice to be wrapped in his arms, feeling protected, warm, loved. Wanted.

"If this was as far as we ever went... I think I'd still choose to be with just you, if that's what it took, sis," he said, kissing my neck, suckling my earlobe. "I'd sail you out here every night, watch the sunset with you, as I held you in my arms... pleasing your little pussy."

That was an extremely tempting offer.

Just laying back and being pleased sounded like a life worthy of a Princess.

Of a Hawthorne.

"You mean it, Malcolm? Even if I never took your cock?"

He shuddered at my words, and I thought at first it was because I sounded like I'd never give up my V to him. But then he spoke in my ear.

"God, hearing you talk like that... it does such things to me, sis," he confessed. But his words weren't necessary, because I felt how his dick throbbed wildly against me. "Yes. God yes, I mean it... I'm crazy about you, Priss. But would you do me a favour? If I never get to have you fully... would you at least watch me jerk off after I finish pleasing you? Just... watch me. And know that it's all because of you that I'm so hard... so horny."

I was eagerly nodding my head. The idea of watching him, knowing it was all my fault, was a delight beyond reason. Beyond words. It was perfect.

"Oh god, that would be so hot," I purred, my ass grinding against his cock, my pussy rubbing eagerly along his fingers. "Malcolm, I wish we'd done this ages ago. You're so good," I murmured.

"Same Priss... god, I was such a fool," he said, burying his head in the crook of my neck, kissing me with a voracious appetite as his hand continued to tease and please my pussy. And it felt so perfectly... safe, comforting and satisfying to be like that. My big brother having opened his good side to me again, and the two of us revelling in each other on the open sea.

"I'll do anything you ask. I just need to keep a hold of you forever," he professed, his undying life expressed like a dam that had just burst.

"Can you... Can you get yourself off while still fingering me? Will that be too much?" I asked, surprised at how breathless and excited I sounded. I was really getting into it. Victor had given me his blessing and encouragement to enjoy the moment, and there was really nothing holding me back from just surrendering to my lust.

I could feel the excitement in Malcolm rise, and his dick pulsate enthusiastically. I know I had to get him to fuck me raw, and cum inside me for the plan to work. But... I couldn't help wanting to draw the moment out, enjoy the day. Enjoy Malcolm's treatment of me.

"God sis, fuck... yes," he said, enthusiastically. "I can do that. Uh... maybe you can lean back on the pillows instead, and I'll get in front of you. Jerk off while I finger you? If, uh... if you don't mind my cum landing on you that is," he said.

"I wouldn't mind," I admitted, my steel eyes meeting his over my shoulder. "Maybe it would make things less... intimidating," I said, using his own words as a confession. "I know this is so wrong but I want you to make it all right."

He visibly shivered with excitement, his handsome face framed by his blonde hair looking utterly smitten. And he nodded to me, leaning in and kissing my lips lovingly, passionately. His tongue sliding over my lips and then between them, as he held me, fingered me. And when, at last, he broke that kiss, he carefully lifted me off him, before getting up.

"Alright, lay back, sis," he instructed me, as we switched spots, only he straddled the seat to face me. His thick, veiny shaft jutting out so hard and ready.

I didn't hide my stare, didn't hold back my interest. I was ravenous for him, and even though I was trying to toy with him, make sure to snare him tight, it was really hard to resist jumping on that dick and giving away the fact that I was definitely not a virgin.

I controlled the impulse to jump his bone, or even to touch it. I just laid back and let his fingers worship my pussy, relaxing into this incestuous little game.

And what a delightful game it was. Watching Malcolm wrap his big, strong hand around that thick cock was delightfully arousing. Seeing him pump that girth up and down as he stared at me, lusting for my body, his eyes darting from my tits to my pussy with such longing... intoxicating. And even as he did so, he kept his fingers teasing my slit, until two of them began to slide up inside me.

"Mmm Priss... you're the most stunning woman I've ever seen," he said, as his dick spurt a tiny bit of pre-cum onto my mons, and his fingers began to pump in and out of me.

His cock was so close, it was such a challenge to stay in place, to not beg him to just tease me with the tip of his dick. He was gorgeous, and now that his over-confident facade had dropped away, I was smitten with him.

"Ah. Ah!" I whimpered as his fingers entered me,

grazed against that inner bundle of nerves. "Right there, Mal."

The excitement on his face as I moaned and begged him to continue, it was so touching. He was eager to please me, even as his cock swelled, throbbing so thick and lewdly as his stroking grew faster, his abs rolling with his increased breathing. And he found that place in me so perfectly as he did it all.

"I'm... I'm gonna cum soon, sis," he moaned, and I could see his balls beginning to tighten, showing it was quite close indeed. "I want to bust all over you... so badly," he moaned.

"I want it!" I moaned as I thrust my hips up just a bit, just enough for his cock to graze against my skin. My eyes rolled back in my head. My lips fell open.

Sparks ignited.

I was completely lost to pleasure, but I forced my gaze back upon his cock. I wasn't willing to miss his finale.

And what a finale it was! The stunning sight of such a well built man, stroking him off, as his thick, long cock began to erupt. Such rich strands of incestuous seed blasting out over me, showering me with his cum. I felt the hot stuff splatter onto my tits with the first shot, and the more that came, the more it plastered over me. Coating my tummy, my mons, while some landed on my inner thighs and even pussy. And all the while his eyes rolled back into his head and he looked blissfully pleased beyond measure. He must've been pent up, because that rain of seed never seemed to end, until finally it began to taper off.

When my orgasm hit me, it hit hard. I had fucked a lot more recently, but I wasn't expecting to be able to bring such a powerful man to his knees. To make him cum so hard, with just the sight of my tits, and the feel of my pussy clenching around his fingers, was an aphrodisiac. I could barely believe my eyes, and I lifted my hips, letting him finger me deeper as I quaked with pleasure.

I glimpsed how some of his cum had splattered on his own hand and fingers, but he never stopped. He kept fingering me masterfully as he blew the last few strands of his cum onto my pussy and mons. And then, with the two of us panting and moaning, he leaned forward, milking the last dollop of seed from his shaft as he sought out my lips.

"S-sorry... I didn't mean to break my word and make you cum," he gasped, before kissing me passionately. Making me relieved to find out that cumming hadn't brought him back to his senses, and sent him spiralling into regret about what we'd just done.

My lips were buzzing with sensation, and I pushed back against him eagerly.

But then I pulled back. If I didn't, I was going to do something I regretted.

"Mal, I have to clean up," I said gently. This would not be our last tryst. I wasn't even planning on it being our last for the day. But I needed to pull away, just enough to make him need to follow me.

He was left hanging, and I saw in his eyes... my worries were for naught. He wanted more. Needed more. Blowing his load onto my tits and pussy wasn't enough to quell his desires for me. And he licked his lips and reluctantly pulled his fingers from my tight slit.

"Okay," he said, breathing heavily, slowly letting his hand slip from his cock, leaving a bead of pearly white seed on the tip.

"I'm going to get a shower," I said as I shifted my legs to the side of the chair to stand. "But... maybe we can watch sunset before heading back home."

I saw the relief on his face at that suggestion, it washed all over him from there. And he smiled up at me before standing, and he was once more looming large.

"I'd really like that, sis," he said, reaching out and brushing his fingers against my wrist, before his eyes were unavoidably drawn down over my cum splattered tits and body. He couldn't help himself. He liked what he saw.

I stood there for a moment. I wanted him to burn this image into his brain.

My fingers tentatively went to my stomach, and I began guiding them upwards, through his cum. They found my breast, squeezing it, before roaming back down and gliding along my slit. I gave him a wicked smile and waited for him to see it before I turned and made my way below deck.

The look on his face at that sight, was something I won't soon forget. Nor the way his just-spent cock twitched with excitement. He was utterly smitten with me, and at that moment I felt like I could do nothing wrong with him. He was enraptured, he craved me. Even after blowing his load he wanted--no, needed--more.

But I wanted him to be unable to help himself, so I pretended like I was oblivious as I headed beneath the deck, into the lavish interior of his yacht. It had all the amenities, and while I might not be able to take a five hour shower, it was spacious and a beautiful white and gold and navy blue tile. It was well decorated, and I knew that I wasn't the first girl to be cleaning off his seed in there.

I hoped, though, that I would be the last.

I turned the solid gold knob to start the warm water flowing as I grabbed one of the pristine white towels and face clothes. I looked at myself in the mirror, my perky tits covered in cum, my grey eyes heavily lidded in the aftermath of my orgasm, my auburn hair messy and wild from the sea salt air.

I looked a little bit wild, my tan deepened, making my eyes look even lighter. I brought my fingers to my mouth, and I tasted my brother's seed, unable to resist, now that I was in private. I then gathered a little more from my mons, and began to finger myself as I waited for the water to fill the air with steam.

"Oh fuck," I gasped, a tremor of an orgasm rolling through me, and I had to pull my seeded fingers out of myself. It wouldn't do to make me cum again, in private. I was on a mission, after all!

I stepped into the warm shower and began to soap up, trying to be quick about it. I was eager to get back to him, even though I knew I needed to make him wait for me.

So far, Victor and I's scheme was working so well. Daddy had been an easy one to win over, he was smitten. Malcolm had taken some more work, but he was no less enraptured. And that meant I now had three of the family men lusting for me, and that felt... oddly powerful. I was the most desired woman in my whole little world on the Hawthorne estate.

It almost felt like a shame to wash away my brother's seed. But as I began to finish up in the shower, I saw the door to the bathroom open. And my very naked, semi-turgid brother stepped into the room.

"I... I couldn't wait any longer," he said to me, conflicted. "I wanted to make sure you... you were still okay. With everything," he said, standing there so tall and dashing.

He was so sweet.

"I can't hear you," I said, raising my voice for effect. "Open the shower door!"

He hesitated only a single moment, and that door opened, the steam flowing out. And I could see him in all his nude glory as he stepped partially in.

"Are you still... okay with everything, sis?" he asked, some worry in his voice. He was terrified he'd frightened me off.

"I... I think so," I said with a half smile, stepping out of the water enough that he could watch beads drip down my nubile form. "I think... I want to do more. If you do. I mean. Do you feel okay with everything?"

His face was a mixture of overjoyed and... disbelief. But he stepped up against me, his hands going to my side, to touch my arm, my hip. He looked down at me with such adoration and desire.

"More than okay," he said, as I felt his dick twitch against me. "I was in denial about what I wanted, and needed, for so long, Priss... but now I accept it, know it. You're all I need and want," he said, leaning down, tilting his head. Kissing me softly.

It was so sweet, and I wrapped my arms around his neck, kissing him back with equal tenderness.

"How long until sunset?" I murmured against his mouth.

He held me, wrapped his arms around me, and we stood there, damp and in love and lust with each other. Until finally he stopped kissing me long enough to answer.

"I don't know. A little while."

"Maybe we could just... hold each other until then? And when the sun starts dipping in the sky, we can head back up and enjoy ourselves? Fully, I mean... I want you to be my first, Mal," I said, the lies coming easy to me now. I knew what I wanted, and I knew I wasn't going to get it if I was honest.

Think me a scheming bitch if you like, but... in truth, it was becoming far less about any idea of inheriting wealth. And more about hoarding the love and affection and desire of the Hawthorne men. And how good it made me feel to have them lust for me, crave me.

And in that moment, the look of excitement and joy on Malcolm's face told me he was more than happy for my little lie.

"God Priss... yes, yes! I'd love that so much," he said, kissing me again, passionately, deeply. And he squeezed me in his strong arms, before pulling away with a grin. He grabbed the towel, and began to dry me off. "Here," he said, "let me help."

I turned off the water, and let him take care of me, pamper me. He was slow and meticulous, treating my body like an object of worship, patting my skin with care. Then he went to grab a bottle of lotion that smelled slightly of vanilla and sugar, and started rubbing that up my legs, over my hips and ass.

"You're a goddess, Priss," he said, as he got down on one knee and thoroughly lotioned up my shapely legs, skirting my pink pussy as he wound upwards to my hips and then tummy. "And I'll pamper you like one every day, if you let me take you out here and escape the world to do so," he professed, before rising up, his strong hands moving to lotion my breasts, shoulders. But lingering on my breasts over long.

It was amazing. His hands were so diligent, rough from his years of sailing and horseback riding, and he just felt so masculine. All the Hawthorne men were masculine in their own ways, of course, but I'd say that Mal was the most traditionally handsome of them all.

"I'm really glad you don't regret it."

He finished up lotioning me at my neck, and then he held me by it, pulling me in and kissing me again. Slow and lovingly this time.

"I could never regret sharing some time with you anymore, sis... my eyes are opened. And I know I have a lot to make up for. So that I can prove I'm worthy of you. Your time. Your love," he said, nuzzling his nose to mine, before taking my hand to lead me towards the master bedroom, with its big bed.

The yacht really was something else. The master bedroom was gold, black and navy, and tastefully appointed. But it also had glorious silk sheets, a huge canopy, and pot-lights overtop it that could change colour. Malcolm put on some classic music, and the lights began to dance to the tempo as we lay back on the bed.

We didn't do anything more than hug and cuddle, talk about our lives, our goals, our dreams. He was full of them, the big picture of what he wanted to do, where he wanted the Hawthorne name to go.

True to his hard working demeanour, he wanted to accomplish much. But not under the wing of father or grandfather. He had been laying the groundwork of his own company, to add to the Hawthorne estate. And I couldn't help but admire his ambition as we cuddled and kissed.

At a point, he even got up to go make me some food. And we laid there, laughing as he fed me sweet morsels, deliciously prepared.

But as the hours slipped by, we saw the orange glow of sunset out one of the large windows of the main bedroom.

"Shall we go up, sister?" he asked me, kissing me, taking my hand.

There was no more asking if he was sure, no more teasing or prolonging things. I'd been waiting with an excited beat to my heart as we relaxed out at sea, but the moment he said that, my head was nodding.

I was more than ready.

I needed him with every fibre of my being.

"I'm so ready, brother."

He smiled and helped me up off the bed. The two of us living like the lavish heirs of the family fortune that we were, strolling about the extravagant bedroom of the yacht, nude and carefree, restrained by no inkling of morality or decency.

He guided me up to the deck again, where the burnt orange sky was beautifully casting its glow down upon us. And I didn't need to do a thing, to see his cock was rigid with excitement, aching for me.

"Oh Priss... this is such a perfect moment," he said, his arms wrapped around me from behind, his dick against my ass as he kissed my shoulder, then up to my neck.

"How should we do this?" I asked innocently, since this *was* my first time and all. My hands roamed up his hips from behind me as my head tilted to the side. It cast my auburn hair over my shoulder, and let him kiss my neck, suckling on it slightly, though not enough to leave a mark.

"Any way you like, sis. I want your first time to be perfect," he said, nibbling my neck, then my ear, ever so slightly. And soon he was turning me around, to face him. The love and lust in his eyes unmistakable. "I want you so bad, sis... I'm so glad I get to be your first. And hopefully... we're each other's last too," he said.

It kind of broke my heart to hear him say that, to keep lying to him, honestly. But I kissed him all the same, my tongue trailing along his lower lip.

"I want to look at you. I want to be able to kiss you while we... make love," I said as sweetly as I could.

Because as guilty as I might've felt, I wanted him. All to myself. Just like Victor and daddy. I was a greedy girl, but I'd learned it from the best. And now it was the Hawthorne's turn to sate my insatiable lust for their attention and affection.

"I'd like that very much, sis," he said with a smile. "I can get on top of you, right here on the deck, show you what it's like to make love," he said so adoringly. But then a light seemed to go off in his head. "Fuck... I'll go get us a condom from the bedroom," he said, beginning to turn.

"Mal," I pouted, grabbing his arm. "Come on. It's just us. I don't want there to be anything between us."

I watched his eyes go wide, and saw his resolve to be responsible melt. And he touched me, caressed my side, my breast.

"I don't either... I just... didn't want to fuck up and..." he swallowed, his dick throbbing against me.

"Mal, it's my first time. I want it to be perfect and pure," I said earnestly, gently beginning to guide him towards the large, built in sofa set that surrounded the fire pit. "I want you to show me what it means to be your woman."

He swallowed anxiously and followed me to that big, plush sofa. The yacht was truly lavish beyond all reason, and as I slid back onto my butt and backside, he followed atop me. The orange glow of the sunset behind him as he loomed over me, his hard, tanned body so stunning to behold as he got into position.

"It has to be pure," he repeated to me, looking down so wide-eyed and smitten. "And there's nothing purer than you, sis. Nothing purer than the love I feel for you. I swear," he said, kissing my lips, the head of his cock teasing against my slit, sending a shiver through us both.

It certainly didn't feel pure, but fuck, it felt good.

My back arched, my hips tilted, that excitement building up inside of me.

"I want you so bad, Mal," I purred, kissing his neck. My heart was beating, my pussy was throbbing with need, and the sunset was painting the sky beautiful shades of orange and pink.

He grasped my hip and breast in his two strong, hard hands. And he lined his cock up with my slit. He was all prepared to tease and ease me into it, but he found that slit was achingly wet the moment his dick touched me. And he moaned with desire.

"God you really do want me too," he said, sounding so relieved, as he began to split the glistening labia of my slit open atop the head of his thick cock. That purple crown stretching me open as he slowly, gingerly, began to insert himself into me.

A whimper escaped me from deep in my throat, and my head tilted back as he began to penetrate me.

My knees were bent, pressed to either side of his hips, my shaved pussy so eager for his thick dick.

"You're so big," I cooed.

And he was. I wasn't blowing smoke up his ass there. Malcolm, like all the Hawthorne men apparently, was well hung. Not only thick and long, but gorgeously shaped. The perfect kind of cock to have slide into you and take your virginity... not that I had it left to give still. But I was so into the moment, it truly felt like my first time again.

"Am I going too fast, sis?" he asked, his chest heaving, as he paused his insertion, with just an inch of his manhood inside me. The rest of that veiny girth throbbing freely as he hesitated.

"No. No, you're perfect." I remembered his words about making other women scream, and though I'm sure some of it was bravado, I had no doubt that if he were to let loose, I'd be happily screaming my climax on his cock.

"Just go slow. Just like that," I said. "I want to feel all of you."

He nodded to me, filled with lust and resolve as he began to push more of himself up inside me. And I kept an extra tight grip on him, to keep the illusion alive and strong that I was a virgin. But with the way he trembled from the tight clench of my slit, I worried I might've overshot.

"F-Fuck sis... you're so tight. God no other girl has felt half so good as you," he husked, as his dick edged into me, slowly filling me all the way up. And he squeezed my breast as the head of his thick dick lodged itself up against my utmost depths.

The sunset dazzled behind him. My arms wrapped around his neck. My thighs pressed against his hips.

"You feel like ecstasy," I whimpered, my grey eyes trained upon his. "I can't believe this is what we've been missing out on."

"We don't have to miss out on it ever again, sis," he said, leaning in and kissing me, as his hips began to rock. His gentle pace for my 'first time' so pleasing. The way his thick cock filled me up, made me mewl and moan beneath him. While he himself groaned and held little of his own pleasured sounds back. The two of us fucking out on the ocean, without regard for anything else.

We'd both gotten off earlier that day, but the hours of cuddling and touching one another had sent our passions into overdrive. It was hard for him to keep going slow, and it was hard for me to resist egging him on. But he was a true gentleman, and he always caught himself before he got carried away.

"I want to feel how much you want me," I said.

He moaned at that, his dick swelling. And he shuddered, trying to restrain himself from going too hard.

"If I do that... I'll hurt you. I don't want to ruin your first time," he said, spurting some pre-cum into me as he kissed me, fondled my breast, and lovingly gazed upon me.

"If it gets too much, I'll say... pillow. I promise. I just want to know," I pleaded, my thighs tightening around his muscular hips. "Please, Mal. I want you to cum in me. I want to feel your passion. No more barriers between us."

He shivered at my words, they obviously kindled such desire in him. And I also saw a flicker of torment, like he was thinking it would be unwise. But in the end, he moaned and kissed my lips, then began to pick up his pace.

"I won't let you down, sis," he promised me, as his pace kept building up. And I got to feel his hard cock pounding into me, faster, harder. Until his balls were slapping against my ass loudly, and he was grunting and panting.

He was fit, and the power between each of his thrusts was mind blowing. I was screaming before I was even close to my orgasm, but when he tried to slow down, I was quick with a, "Don't stop!"

Virgins could like it rough too, I imagined.

If he was doubting me, he never showed it. He was just committed to giving me what I wanted. And he kept that hard, rough pace going up, fucking me wildly. He made me scream, just as he'd bragged, and he was loving every moment of it. His body glistening in the orange light, my poor little wet pussy singing with joy as he rammed his dick up into it.

"Never having another girl again... just you, Priss. God I swear it!" he shouted out, as he claimed me so ravenously, his hard fingers sinking into my supple breast tightly.

"I know! I know!"

My pussy was starting to twitch and tighten with that instinctive response, my body coiling around his in preparation. I knew I wasn't going to last that much longer, but I had to hold off.

"I want to cum together," I confessed.

He gasped and shuddered.

"I'm so close... I can't hold it off much longer anyhow," he confessed to me. "Cum for me, sis... cum on my cock," he begged me, as he rutted into me hard, fast. Made me scream as he let out his own roar. And he tried to maintain control, but he was swelling up, and I felt his dick erupting as he shuddered through his wild thrusts.

And the intense orgasm he had managed to conjure up more of his virile seed, firing it off into me atop his wild thrusts.

I let go, let go of all sense of reason or decency as I came on my brother's cock. He was enraptured with me, but I was enraptured with him, too. A part of me knew it was all a ploy, but my goals had shifted, and I wasn't going to be content with just getting knocked up and then letting the Hawthornes beg me for cash or pussy. I wanted a family, and with each man I bedded, that need only grew stronger.

That blissful thought tore through just as the mutual orgasm did. And Malcolm and I screamed and moaned, my pussy gushing honey around his shaft, coating his balls, as we twitched and writhed.

And he never ceased thrusting until after his dick had been drained of every last spurt. And I had every moment of orgasmic ecstasy squeezed from my pussy. And only then did he collapse atop me, huffing and panting, kissing me wildly.

"Oh Priss... I love you so much," he professed.

"I love you, Mal," I said, wrapping my arms around his neck and holding him against my breast. It was almost comforting, in a way. Just letting us lay there, intertwined, our bodies sinfully connected.

It was filthy, but it was also sweet. He kissed me

lovingly, and we made out and caressed each other until the sun was truly set and the night descended on us. Only when the chill of evening began to make our naked flesh bump did it occur to us that we had to get back. We'd been gone all day.

Five

Malcolm got me my clothes, and an extra robe to help wrap around me to keep me warm, and then he turned the yacht around to take us back home.

I grabbed another quick shower as we made our way back to shore, and while we hadn't caught a single fish, neither of us would say our trip had been unsuccessful. And when I joined him on deck again, he was teaching me about the safest way to make it back in the dark, and all the things I should keep an eye out for.

Which was helpful, considering the second I got back, one of the servants informed me that I was summoned by my father. I was to see him in his room immediately.

"Thank you for today, Malcolm," I said as I tugged

my summer jacket a little tighter around me. I wasn't expecting to be gone until well after dark, but I still brought a change of clothes. I had no idea if he might've just ripped them off me, after all.

"It's my pleasure, Priss," he said to me, smiling so sincerely. And I could tell he was aching to kiss me goodbye, but... with the servants around, he restrained himself. "Maybe we can take another ride tomorrow... or whenever you like," he said, eager for more of me.

"I'll send you a message as soon as I can slip away." I promised him that, and I meant it.

It was a really great day.

I blew him a kiss before I turned, practically skipping up to my room. I quickly changed into an evening dress. I chose a simple, black dress that hugged my curves and dipped down far in the back, and had a sweetheart cut in front to show off my cleavage. I paired it with a pearl necklace and earrings, along with a pair of silk thigh highs and some black heels. I thought I looked very elegant, with my hair pulled up out of my face, and started towards Father's room.

When I got there, one of the servants was waiting at the door.

"Looking lovely this evening, madam," was all he said, as he opened the door and I passed through. Father's suite was lavish and beautiful. It was basically a house within the greater mansion itself. He had his own living area, dining room, bedroom, a walk-in closet that was bigger than some houses, and a bathroom that dwarfed even that.

And as I stepped in, I heard the soft, romantic music, and saw that an extravagant dinner was waiting on the table as the door was shut and locked behind me.

"There you are," came my Father's voice, as he smiled down at me, dressed in his finest, looking so dashing. "I was worried you were upset with me," he said, as he descended from the stairs that led up to the second level of his suite, and then to the rooftop pool.

"Of course not!" My hand flittered to my chest before I ran to him, wrapping my arms around him as he reached the bottom of the stairs. "I feel closer to you than ever before."

His arms went around me in return, and rather shamelessly went down my back, to cup my ass as we embraced. He kissed my neck, my shoulder, squeezed me.

"I am so glad to hear that," he said. "I haven't been able to get you and what we did out of my mind. I feared... you were having regrets. Or were just upset with me, for my careless risk with where I deposited my seed," he said, sounding ever so formal, as ever.

"I'm your little girl, aren't I? Isn't it only fair that you show me what it is to be a woman?"

I was getting high on my own intoxication, with how much the men of my family were drawn to me. Even though I'd cum so many times already that day, I was ready for more.

He smiled at me wryly, kissed my lips and squeezed my backside.

"You have no idea how much of a relief it is to hear you say that, my sweet little girl," he murred, caressing my backside. "Oh, what a restless night I had without you in my bed. Can I not persuade you to spend the night this time? I've prepared such a meal, with wine. Anything you'd like," he remarked, kissing me again, as I felt his manhood twitching with excitement.

"I think that sounds lovely, though I've had a long day, so I will need to at least get *some* beauty rest," I teased him, glancing over at the table. My stomach growled as if on cue, which was rather unlady-like, and I giggled. "Oops. Malcolm and I only ate light today so I wouldn't get seasick. I guess my hunger's catching up on me now."

He smiled at me, relieved by my answer. And we disentangled--mostly-- but his hand remained on my ass as he guided me to a chair, then pulled it out for me like a gentleman, helping me seat myself. He placed one of the fancy napkins over my lap for me, then popped the cork on the wine, pouring us both up some.

"I'm so relieved. I have to head out in the morning on a business trip. And I was petrified that I might not get any more time alone with my favourite girl," he said, before kissing my hair then making his way to his seat.

"Will you be gone very long?" I asked as I got settled in, crossing my legs daintily.

"Hopefully no. But to be honest, the idea of another night without you... felt dreadful," he said with a smile as he sipped his wine, and uncovered his meal, to let the steam out. "If I couldn't track you down tonight, I was going to invite you along to come with me. Though it wouldn't be a terribly interesting business trip."

"Lucky I got back when I did, then. For both of us." I followed suit with him, unveiling the sumptuous meal of meat and vegetables he had sautéed up for us. It was my favourite meal five years ago, but I'd forgive him for that. He must have asked especially for it, since the staff know my tastes better than I do.

I took a sip of wine, smiling down the table at him.

"For tonight, then, I'll be your wife?"

The spark of joy on his stern face was my reward. And he raised his glass to me.

"To you then. My precious little girl. My stunning wife," he said, a grin forming on his face. "Oh, and that reminds me... I have a gift for you. After dinner," he said.

"You do know how to build suspense, love," I said casually as I began to eat. It reminded me of how this came to be my favourite meal. The finishing butter was exquisite on the expensive cut of meat, and it was charred in all the right places, tender in the centre. It was delicate and delightful, and I began to eat a little quicker than I wanted to.

Father and I ate our meal and actually chatted, had a lovely conversation. I truly did feel like his wife, taking the spot of my own departed mother. And as the meal was done, he came to me, offered me his hand and helped me up out of my seat.

"I know it's greedy of me, but how I wish I could hoard you to myself like this all the time. Regardless of what the rest of the family or staff thinks of my sweet little girl in my quarters all the time," he said, as he guided me towards his lavish bedroom.

It wasn't a lot of wine, but I felt a pleasant hum in my body, and I *was* excited for a present. Outside of birthdays and Christmas, he hadn't gotten me anything in years, and it was as if I'd suddenly been awoken to something I was deeply missing.

"Close your eyes," he said with a smile as he went and got a box from his nightstand. And I did so. He came to me then, and I felt something cool touch my chest, lodging at my cleavage. "You can open them now," he said, and I looked down to see the most exquisite, lavish necklace I'd ever beheld in my life.

It had to have cost a million dollars, at least. And it was right there, perched atop my tits.

There were no words.

Literally, nothing. Not a sound.

My mouth opened, my knees quivered, my eyes began to tear, but still, not a noise peeped from between my lips. I just looked at him in shock and awe.

"So you like it?" he asked, a burgeoning smile on his face as he reached up and caressed my cheek. "It's not the only thing I got for you this night, but... it is the most expensive piece," he said, before gesturing to the table, which was laden with jewelry boxes. Easily a dozen of them. "I set out to get you just one, but... I got carried away. The necklace. Earrings. Rings. Bracelets. Anklets, even a little jewelled belt," he said.

"D-dad, holy shit, this is too much!" I finally found my words, and I was stripped of all cunning, forgetting our little game outright. I was feeling spoiled, actually spoiled. I know that as a rich potential heiress, my entire life is like being spoiled. But in that moment?

Yea, if I wasn't wet before, I was then.

He came to me, kissed my shoulder, neck, caressed my ass.

"Look through them. Try them on. Any you don't like? I will find another to replace it," he said with a smile. "There is nothing too lavish for my beautiful little daughter-wife," he said with a playful grin. "Nothing I wouldn't spend to make you a little happier."

"Daddy, you didn't have to do this. It's so much," I said, going to one of his standing mirrors and looking at myself in it. I took off my pearls, tilting from side to side in order to watch the diamonds sparkle in the dim light. "Wow..."

He began to open the boxes, coming to me as I eyed that fat sparkling necklace atop my tits, putting on a bracelet, then another. Slipping in the earrings as I watched myself become a lavishly bejewelled princess.

"I wanted to," he said, kissing the back of my neck again, then bending down, to wrap an anklet around me. "You reminded me of what it's like to let myself feel love and pleasure again. After I'd forgotten it all, my little Princess Priscilla," he said, before rising up.

I'm not so emotionally devoid that I'd lie about the fact that I began to cry, then. Tears of joy. He really did move me, in that moment, and made me realize the power I had. Victor was trying to consolidate power for us, but I was always the one that could bring our family together, and make our extravagant estate a home.

"Dad... I love it. It's beyond..." I trailed off, feeling myself get choked up.

I was covered in more glittering jewels than a Pharaoh, and as I looked in the mirror I watched as my Father wrapped his arms around my waist, attaching that final, gold belt, before squeezing me in an embrace.

"It's no more than you deserve. Far less in fact," he said, kissing my neck, eyeing me in the mirror. "I wanted to buy you some new clothes too, but... perhaps another time, when we can go together. And you need more bikini sets like that one that... awoke me to reality," he said.

I smiled at our reflections, feeling such warmth flood my heart.

"I'd enjoy that. Being your little dress up doll," I admitted. "I wouldn't mind some more diamond bikinis either." I was teasing on that, but I knew he'd readily bejewel me head to toe if I wished it. "I want to thank you. I know I don't have to. But... I want to. Will you teach me to please you with my mouth?"

His eyes flared open widely at that, and his smile grew again into a broad grin. He let his hands caress over my taut, flat tummy where--by now I hoped--life was taking root. And he nuzzled my ear, kissed it, then murmured softly.

"Of course... and I will bless you with a dozen diamond bikinis for it," he said, his dick throbbing against my ass. "You are such a good little girl, my Princess. You will look ever so lovely on your knees, with my cock in your mouth," he husked.

I gasped, his words sending a lightning bolt through my body, igniting a fire within my core.

I turned to face him, my grey eyes lifted to meet his.

"Where do you want me?"

He groaned with desire, kissing my lips and then licking his own.

"Right here, in front of the mirrors," he said, gesturing around at the semi-circle of lavish mirrors that would let him stare at me from every angle. "But first... take off your dress. Wear nothing but the jewelry," he said, teeming with excitement for me.

"No heels?" I asked as I turned around, getting his help with the zipper and the belt so that I could let the dress slide down my long legs until the expensive garment was little more than a puddle on the floor.

He trembled with anticipation, letting his hands slide down over my figure, caressing my hips, waist, ass and thighs, then back up to fondle my breasts a little.

"Keep the heels," he said, before retracting his hands, undoing his jacket and tossing it away. Then after that, he began to work open his belt. "God, look at you. Beyond perfection," he said, eyeing me directly, then in the mirror from every angle.

I wasn't self conscious, and let him stare at my tanned, youthful figure. I knew it wasn't going to last forever, but while I was in my prime, I had full intentions of enjoying it. Enjoying my men in as many different ways as I could.

"What about the thigh highs?" I asked as I began helping him with his belt.

He licked his lips, staring longingly at my tits as I opened up his belt, undid his pants and began to peel them down. And all the while he unbuttoned his shirt, and peeled it back off him to toss it atop his discarded jacket.

"Keep those too... just the little accent to your beauty. The jewels and such, to accentuate your naturally gorgeous form," he said, licking his lips as I helped tug his pants and underwear down, to let his thick, veiny dick spring up. That gloriously thick cock that he'd passed onto his two sons.

My hand wrapped around it, testing its strength.

"Did you jerk off thinking about me in my bikini after your meeting?"

The heat of Father's cock was so high, and his dick pulsated in my grasp. He was primed and ready, so horny for me it was astounding. That cock felt iron-shod in my hand, lacking none of the size or solidity of his two sons when they claimed me, showing age wouldn't keep them all from satisfying me for the rest of my days.

"God yes, I did," he said, swallowing as he moaned from my mere touch. His hand caressed my hair, "I couldn't think or do anything until I'd tried to do something about it... but I kept getting interrupted before I could finish. And then I knew I had to have you," he said, licking his lips.

I began to get down on my knees, my legs slightly spread so he could get a view of my pussy and ass.

"Daddy, I know it's so wrong, but hearing you talk like that makes my little pussy so wet," I confessed, my face mere inches from his throbbing dick. "It makes me want to spread my legs for you, let you get off in me, knock me up... Whatever you want."

He shivered at my words, and his dick leaked pre-cum in response. He moaned and guided my head in towards his cock, letting me feel it's veiny hot length against my cheek, before my lips were brought to the tip.

"Dammit, princess... do you know what you're saying? God, how I'd love to treat you absolutely and without reservation as my wife. Nothing would make me happier than to plant another heir inside you... my, how perfect such a child would be," he groaned.

"So do it," I said, swiping my tongue around his crown. "You're the head of the family. And I want it," I reminded him, my grey eyes trained to his face. "Just think of me, all swollen with your baby."

His dick strained so thickly in my hand, and he moaned from my words. His fingers knit into my hair, and he kept me close, guiding me gently to lick and taste his cock.

"Oh fuck, princess... I want that so badly," he shuddered, his hips pushing forward a bit. "I already came in you once... I was so worried you were upset at me for that. That you'd want me to have it taken care of... but I should've known what a good little girl you are," he said. "But my god... what would people say? Here, lick and kiss," he instructed.

I followed his instructions, let his hands and body guide me. My mouth was kept too full to respond, but the way I moved my head, the squeeze my hands gave his hips, that'd hopefully be enough to assuage his nerves. I mean, we were rich enough that it really didn't matter what people said. We could buy off the ones that mattered, and ignore the rest that didn't.

Besides, I barely left the estate, so it wasn't like anyone outside of staff and business partners might get an inkling of the incestuous intrigues that fill our Hawthorne Halls.

But I knelt there a long while, worshipping my Father's cock, lavishing it with such attention. And I was rewarded with a nice, salty spurt of his pre-cum onto my tongue as I sucked Daddy off. Until finally, he guided my mouth off his shaft, and slid that glistening member along my cheek as he guided me to kiss his balls.

"I can save this load to dump in your tight little pussy then, princess... is that what you want?" he asked me, breathless amid his moans of pleasure.

"Yes," I panted, my tongue bathing his sack with such appreciation and desire. His cock throbbed against my face, messing up my subtle makeup, but I knew that would only make me more arousing to him. I didn't rush, I took my time as I paid my gratitude to his body, worked out all those long pent up daddy issues on his cock and balls.

He shuddered with anticipation after my confession, and he guided me to stand up, taking my hand into his.

"You are..." he was speechless, but he kissed me, held me. And we made out passionately. My days now were spent passing between Hawthorne men, absorbing their lusts and passions, being treated so decadently. I was living my best life.

"I want you to lay back, princess. Beg me to plant a child in you," he said, as he guided me towards the massive bed.

My long legs were graceful in my heels, and I kneeled on the bed for a moment, letting him look over my body as I spread my legs for him. My torso lowered to the exquisite sheets, wiggling my ass before I rolled over onto my back.

My legs were spread wide, my pussy swollen and pink with arousal and overuse.

"Daddy. I need you to fill me with your cum and make me a real Hawthorne lady," I said, obediently.

He groaned as he watched my sultry little display, and he followed after me, climbing up on the bed on his knees. He got over me, grasping my knees, helping part them even wider as his hard dick jutted out so needfully, glistening with my saliva.

"However many virile years I have left in me... I

want to spend them all planting new Hawthornes in you, princess," he husked, leaning down, kissing me passionately and fondling a breast, as his dick pressed against my pussy, and our loins ground together.

I relaxed back on the bed with my legs spread as wide as I could manage them. My grey eyes trailed down his body to his cock, and I made my pussy lips give his shaft a long, wet kiss.

"Don't make me wait, daddy. I need it."

He shivered and moaned, and drew his hips back, lining up his dick with my slit.

"You've got me so worked up, princess. Daddy's not sure how long he can last in that exquisite little pussy of yours," he warned me, as he began to push his cock up inside me. The feeling of my wet, warm pussy engulfing his shaft again making his eyes roll back and causing him to moan so loudly.

I rocked my hips forward.

"Fuck me. Make me yours again. I need it so bad, Daddy," I pleaded, my body calling out for his, craving his cock. I was turning into a real naughty nympho, but I didn't care about that at all at the moment. The only thing on my mind was his cum, and how much I needed to know that I could get him off, again and again.

He shoved his cock all the way up inside me with a

final jab, and he moaned aloud. He squeezed my breast, holding himself up on his other arm as he began to thrust into me, making my tits jiggle, his balls slapping to my ass.

"Ohhh princess... fuck, take it. Take Daddy's cock and cum like the good little girl you are," he grunted out.

He warned that he wouldn't last long, but that must have been relative. He had just as much stamina as his sons, and I was crying out long before he reached his peak. It wasn't until I was racked by my second orgasm that he showed signs of losing control.

I clung to him, my lavish jewelry sparkling in the light of his room, my skin glistening with sweat as he made my young body twist and twitch with pleasure.

"Daddy's cumming princess," he gasped out, his lean, hard body shuddering as his dick tensed up, throbbed, and then... more of that rich, thick, proven-virile seed of his flooded into me. This time, he was quite purposely trying to knock me up, to plant his seed. And he revelled in it so much as he shoved his dick in all the way and implanted it there, locking his load within me as he trembled.

I held him in my arms as I trembled. It was so good. I felt so spoiled, so taken care of. My needs were being met in a way that I'd never realized possible, and

I wanted to enjoy every single second of it. My legs wrapped around him, not eager for him to leave me, as my fingers stroked his spine with such affection.

He held me in return, caressed my body, showered me with kisses.

"Ohh princess, you've made me happier than I've ever been," he confessed to me, his dick still locked deep within. He kissed me some more, lavishing such affection on me. "I have to fuck and rut you again before you leave this bedroom. Know that there's no way to escape it," he rumbled to me, so insistent.

"Wake me up on your dick, then, Daddy. You can be my morning alarm," I purred in his ear, the exhaustion of the day beginning to weigh upon me.

He kissed along my shoulder, to my neck, then nibbled it so much like Malcolm had, before tonguing my ear.

"Oh I will, princess. I promise you that," he said," as we touched and made out a while longer, my tired body slowly winding down until we disentangled, and he wrapped the exquisite sheets over me, cuddling up against me, holding me in his arms as we settled in for the night.

Six

It was the first full night I'd ever spent in bed with someone else. Victor and I had been together a while, but we'd never had the luxury of just... chilling out, cuddling and sleeping together through a whole night. Not unless we wanted to take a big risk in getting caught!

So that night with Father was... special. And the safest, most secure night's sleep I ever had.

It had little to do with his glamorous room, and all the fine furniture. It was about being held, and loved. Desired and wanted. Being kept safe and secure.

So when I finally woke up, I was in a very good mood.

For more reasons than one. Because when I did begin to stir to consciousness, Daddy's cock was already a couple inches inside me. My pussy damp from some dream I was having, his shaft stretching me open, sinking into me as he moaned softly into my ear between kisses of my neck.

I moaned in return. I wasn't awake enough to try to play games, my sleepy eyes still closed against the intrusion of wakefulness.

It was pleasure without thought, without rationality, as my pussy spread for him. I was so eager, without even being conscious of it, and my hips bucked back towards him.

We were both on our sides, spooning into each other, his cock sinking in deep and impaling me. It was the most delightful wakeup call of my life, and even in my semi-conscious state I was moaning as Daddy's hips began to rock, his dick pumping into me at such a delightful pace.

"Ohhhh, Princess..." he moaned into my ear, his hand gripping my hip as he fucked me.

A shiver of delight went through me at his husky, masculine voice. He was so aroused, and it really didn't matter that I was his daughter. Maybe that made it even hotter for him. I had to admit, it really heightened the kink for me.

So I didn't hold back as I shifted, grabbing the fine

sheets as I pushed my pussy onto him, taking his shaft so deep.

He groaned even deeper at my eager willingness, and we ground and rut each other so lovingly. His hand slipped from my hip, traveling up over my stomach, "Fuck Princess... you need to carry Daddy's baby in you, don't you?" he groaned, before his hand continued up to cup and fondle my breast. My thick ass quaked with each pump of his steely hard morning-wood cock.

One of the other things about never being able to spend the night with a lover is that I had never experienced how *hard* a cock gets in the morning. Or how long he could last.

I was still caught between sleep and wake, but my conscious and subconscious were united by desire.

"Yes, Daddy," I groaned out, my entire body shivering with my confession. "I need it so bad."

"Ahhh, Princess... you're such a good little girl. Though your tits feel anything but little now," he rumbled with approval, pinching my nipple between two of his knuckles as his cock pumped into me harder, faster. The pace of our early morning rutting casual by comparison to the night before, but still so passionate.

He kissed my shoulder, licked my neck, bit my earlobe as he spurt pre-cum into me.

He was taking his time with me, and edging me towards a slower building orgasm. I could feel my body begin to coil, but any time I risked nearing that precipice, he changed his tempo. He was so in tune with my body, knew just how to drive me wild. Malcolm and Victor were skilled, there was no doubt about that, but Father had decades of experience on either of them, and he was using those talents to take me to a new level.

"You're so big," I cooed out.

And it was true, all the Hawthorne men were big. And satisfying. And telling them always made them pleased to fuck me even more.

"And you're so tight, Princess... fuck, Daddy's never had such a tight, satisfying pussy before," he groaned, squeezing me in his two strong arms, holding me against him as he pumped into me. His bedroom, massive as it was, filled with the sounds of her moaning, our bodies wetly slapping together.

I started to gasp for breath, and he slowed down, grinding his dick into me more sensuously.

"Not until I say so," he ordered, and a thrill went down my spine. I loved being under his control, knowing that before long, he'd send me rocketing over the edge. But not a moment before he allowed it.

My pussy sucked him in deeper and I ground in against him, my thighs pressed together to squeeze his cock even harder.

All his years of experience paying off, working me like a skilled musician plays an instrument, making my body sing with pleasure and desire. I felt my body rock with each thrust he made, and as I was panting and trembling, unable to push back at him anymore, he made up for it by pumping into me harder, faster.

"So close, pretty Princess Priscilla... Daddy's getting so close," he groaned into my ear deliciously.

It nearly tipped me over, just those sweet, filthy words. I knew how wrong it was. How kinky. How I could literally tell no one outside of the estate about the forbidden things I was getting up to within our walls.

But that all just made me shiver with excitement. I managed to hold back, though.

"Daddy, cum in me," I pleaded. "I need it so bad."

He shuddered at my words, his dick swelling thickly in my pussy, and that moan he gave told me all I needed to know that he was no less in love and lust with me than I was with him. And so as he thrust into me wildly, he struck that perfect tempo, and my body was helpless as he let loose a roar.

"Cum for Daddy baby girl!" he growled out, as he began to shoot off his thick, creamy load of seed deep into my pussy. All that virile seed, which had been proven by fathering his sons, flooding into my pussy and womb, ensuring that if none of the other guys had done it yet... surely it must be my Daddy who was going to knock me up.

I screamed.

I just let loose. It didn't matter anyways. The Estate was well built, and his room was practically soundproof. I had no shame, even if the entire place could hear me. He'd toyed with me so much, so exquisitely, that there was no holding back or hiding my pleasure.

My pussy gushed around him, sweet honey pouring over his sack and thigh as he pounded his cum deep into me.

And so we lay there, the two of us trembling as we came simultaneously. His seed filling me, his dick twitching inside me, making me feel so loved and held. And we wound down, ever so slowly, from our blissful heights.

He was panting as he held me, his hand still

clutching my breast, and finally as he caught his breath, he began to kiss my neck again.

"Dammit, Princess... I wish I didn't need to head off for that work trip today," he groaned.

"I know." I was sad about it too, honestly. But it did give me time to get ready for Uncle Arthur's visit. He was going to be returning soon, and he always came around for a visit after he got back from a trip. Father was disgruntled that he'd be missing his brother, though that was long forgotten with the grip my pussy had on him.

"It'll give us time to miss one another, though," I said with a soft smile, my fingers roaming over his hand lovingly.

"Mmmm," he kissed my neck again softly, holding me tightly. "And I will be missing you Princess... you and that perfect body. Those exquisite tits. That tight little pussy... every bit of you the finest imaginable," he groaned appreciatively, before finally, reluctantly peeling himself from me, leaving my pussy gaping and drooling his seed as he pulled away to get ready.

"I can send you pictures while you're gone?" I offered, a wicked smile on my lips. "That way you won't have time to have regrets. I don't want you to think you were just pent up and find some random woman to take to bed, after all."

He was making his way to the closet as I said that and he paused to look back at me, a wry smile on his handsome, paternal face.

"I like the sound of that. Little reminders of my girl to keep me from straying," he remarked. "Not that any old woman could suffice now that I've had you, Princess. You are without compare. And I think even if I tried to sate my needs elsewhere now, I would only be left longing for you even more."

I smiled as I shifted to the edge of the bed, watching him. I'd taken the jewels off before falling asleep, and so I was completely nude before him. It didn't bother me. I was getting a lot more comfortable being nude, really.

"Will you bring me and the boys back a present?"

He was picking out some items from his closet, a nice shirt, an exquisite tie, some fetching pants. But he carried on talking with me as he did so.

"For you at least," he said with a smile in my direction. "Do you have any requests, Princess? Anything at all. Just say the word," he said.

"I don't know, I was just thinking of something that might help bring us together as a family," I said, my words measured. "I mean, I think it'd be better to have us all in good spirits when things get out about us, right? So being warm to Victor and Malcolm... I think that'd be good for all of us."

He seemed thoughtful about that, pondering it as he did his tie with such a practiced hand, then pulled on his sharp blazer over top of it.

"I see what you mean. It would be best to have everyone... contented, in case word gets out about our new arrangement together," he said, putting on some fine shoes, before stepping out towards me, reaching to caress my hair. "You are as wise as you are beautiful, my Princess," he said dotingly.

"I'll text you with some ideas as they come to me," I said with a chipper smile, nuzzling into his hand.

He leaned down and kissed my forehead tenderly.

"Text me with more than that, Princess," he said with a hint of a lusty rumble before he smiled and headed out. "Be ready for my return. I will be missing you terribly, Princess!" he called to me before he was gone, and I was left nude in my father's bed.

I took my time, getting dressed. I wasn't in a huge rush. It wasn't like I had a job, other than being rich and trying to get my family to knock me up.

By the time I had my skirt and blouse back on, my cache of diamond jewelry carefully put back in their boxes for transport, it was mid morning. Staff bustled around as

I walked back to my room, though they mostly didn't pay me much mind, outside of the regular pleasantries that I returned. They were busy, and I didn't enjoy wasting any of their time, and they appreciated that, well enough.

When I opened the door to my room, though, I couldn't hold back my cry of surprise, and one of the maids came running.

Seven

" It's nothing!" I said as I tried to usher her away.

"Miss! Your scream was not for nothing!"

She tried to get around me, to look in my room, and I dropped one of the jewelry boxes as I tried to cut her off.

"No, no. Seriously. I just forgot that..." Fuck, my brain was moving slow after the morning sex. "I forgot that I'd left some food in here the other day, the smell startled me."

"I'll fetch it, Miss, don't worry!" she said as she practically pushed past me, and I followed after. Though my room looked -- and smelled -- perfectly fine.

"I don't smell anything, Miss," the maid said, looking at me with confused, brown eyes.

"Oh. My mistake," I said, trying to guide her back to the door. "Maybe I'm sleepwalking. Who knows!"

She gave me a look like I was crazy, but she went to the door, bending over and picking up the diamond bracelet that Father had given me.

"This is very beautiful, Miss. You should be more careful with it," she chided as she handed it back, and I nodded.

"Of course, Monica. Thank you!"

I shut the door behind her, just in time to hear Victor's giggle come from my closet.

"You asshole," I said as I tossed open the closet door, the white and gold glittering in the midday sun that cascaded through my gossamer curtains.

Victor stepped out, nude as the day he was born. His pale but sculpted body capturing the sunlight beautifully, as his impressive manhood sat soft but still gorgeous. And he came towards me, with that cocky, amused grin on his face to touch my waist and take my hand, his kiss landing upon my neck.

"Good morning to you too, sis," he said with a playful tease in his voice. "What can I say? I just couldn't wait to see you again. Didn't even have time to put on some clothes!"

"Oh my God, how many of the staff did you flash today?" I asked with a roll of my eyes. Still, I couldn't hide my amused grin, and so I turned my back on him, heading to my vanity to begin putting my new jewelry away.

Victor just casually strutted across the room over beside me, folding his arms as he leaned back against the wall, watching me.

"I didn't walk all the way over here naked, silly sis. My clothes are in the closet," he said, hooking a thumb back towards it. "I came to surprise you, but it seems a certain Miss Priss was out all night," he said with a saucy smile.

"You can't be mad at me just because I'm too good at the task you gave me." I laid out all the boxes of jewelry that Father had bought me, opening them up, one by one. "What do you think?"

Victor's brows rose, and he stared at my array of dazzlingly expensive jewelry.

"Holy shit..." he said, reaching out and touching some of them. "Damn, you **are** good. Too good almost," he was stunned by my collection. "Dad can barely be talked into handing over anything... and you got him to turn over a treasure trove."

"He's headed out on his trip and I suggested he return with something for all of us. The whole family.

Since it's bound to be awkward when our arrangement comes out," I said, as I ran my fingers down over Victor's chest affectionately. "Malcolm was putty in my hands--and mouth as well."

Victor's cock twitched to life at my touch, it never took much from me to make the Hawthorne men throb after all. And he eyed me with unmasked desire.

"How's dad buying us all a gift make it easier when you and I come out though?" he asked, slow on the uptake, but then his head was clearly focussed on my tits and other physical assets.

My fingers trailed down his chest, over his abs, then wrapped around his cock.

"Victor, love. We don't really want to rule with fear, do we? I know how much this family situation has sucked, and the distance between all of us. But I don't think that's inevitable," I said softly. "All the Hawthorne men have forbidden tastes. It's mutually assured destruction for anyone to talk about what's going on in these halls. So why not make this estate a *home* for us and our baby?"

I knew it would be a... delicate topic to broach with Victor, since he had his own ideas of how things would go down. But with my dainty hand wrapped around his cock, beginning to stroke him with practiced precision--I knew that shaft so well, after-all--his mood was suitably improved.

"Uh," he started to try and talk, but my deft hand motions had set him off kilter. And his manhood throbbed wildly against my touch as he blinked away his confusion. "So you're saying..." he moaned, "what are you saying, Priss?" he asked, his brow furrowed a bit as his breathing grew heavier.

"I'm saying that this might be the thing that helps all of us pool our resources and stop looking at each other as a threat or an enemy," I said, kissing his throat. "Imagine. Malcolm wants to start his own business, add to the Hawthorne estate, and you know he's likely to be successful. If we push him too hard, we might get the inheritance, but nothing that he earns on his own. Father's business has always been steady, and I'm sure his business associates will be more eager to come by for meetings with me traipsing around."

I began to stroke him in earnest, peppering his chest with kisses and licks as I spoke.

"We wouldn't just be getting the estate, the inheritance, if we pooled everything together. You and I would be set up for the rest of our lives. And our child, too. Riches beyond reason. And your full time job can be taking care of their swollen princess."

Victor might've been the toughest sell of all.

Because he had his plan, and when Victor had a plan... he hated to not see it though. He was stubborn and determined in that way. But my hand and lips worked to help him see things my way, to alter the plan... just a bit. And he shuddered against me as he licked his lips.

"Sis... I was really looking forward to parading around this place, with you as my bride... openly," he said, his voice thick with lust and pleasure, a groan spilling from his mouth as he reached up to caress my hair.

"It's all going to come out, Victor. You and I know that," I said with a warm smile. "And that's what I want, too. It's just... I don't want to be a queen, lording over everyone else. I'm thinking more... Hedonistic Hawthornes, rather than Flowers in the Attic."

He moaned at my attentions, his cock pulsating with desire. And he caressed my cheek, my hair, he kissed my forehead and nuzzled against me.

"Fuck... I dunno sis," he groaned, his dick leaking precum onto my wrist as I stroked him. "That's gonna be a hard one to balance... Malcolm never liked sharing. Dad is so used to being on top of everything..." he grunted out.

"You let me deal with them. You're the one with the real power here. You're the only one that knows that I'm about to break your father and your brother in two when I reveal that neither of them was *really* my first, because Victor corrupted me first," I reminded him, a sinister grin to my voice. "Think of how spoiled I'll be. How spoiled we'll be. Father already agreed to get something for the whole family, after all, and I want you to choose."

Victor was struggling, he could barely keep his eyes open as he moaned softly from my touch. And he caressed me, kissed me.

"Fuck sis... I can't even think right now. Let alone come up with some big gift idea for the family... not that that kinda thing is my speciality anyhow," he said. "All I've wanted for ages is you. To have you," he said with a moan.

"You have me," I reminded him with a lick of my tongue. "Dad's gone on his trip. Uncle Arthur doesn't get here until tomorrow. Malcolm's already headed out on his boat by now. Why don't we spend the day together. I promise I'll give you time to think between fuckings."

He shuddered all over, my sensual touches and licks driving him crazy, robbing him of his greatest strength: his brilliant mind. And he licked his lips, swallowing heavily as he tried to process what I was saying.

"Dammit sis... you gotta suck my cock to start. You

have to," he groaned, his hand on my shoulder gently nudging me down.

I wasn't interested in resisting. I wanted to taste his masculinity on my tongue, and so I kneeled before him in my skirt, stockings, heels and blouse of the night before. I looked every bit the professional woman, except for how eagerly my mouth was moving down my brother's stiff cock.

I moaned against his shaft, the vibration traveling down his length.

Victor's eyes rolled back into his head, and he groaned deeply as I swallowed his thick girth. His hand ran through my dark hair, caressing and holding me. He swelled in my mouth, straining my jaw open wide as my chin felt his heavy balls.

"Do you know how hard it has been having to share you with them? Fuck I've missed you sis," he moaned out, his ripped body tensing up. All those sculpted muscles bulging.

And I knew his feelings intimately. As much as I was enjoying my time with Malcolm and Father... there really was something about Victor. He and I were so compatible, we had such an easy relationship. I didn't have to put on airs for him, pretend I was someone I'm not. He loved me for who and what I was.

But my time with the others convinced me that I

couldn't be as cruel and calculating as he might want me to be.

So instead I bobbed my head up and down Victor's shaft, swirling my tongue along his veiny girth, and did what I do best. What I enjoy the most. Sucking, fucking, enjoying cock, and pleasing the Hawthorne men.

Victor grunted from my attentions, spurting precum onto my tongue and to the back of my throat. His girth so stiff and needy, his body so hard and primed.

It didn't have all the strength as a freshly awoken morning wood, but it was more than hard, and eager for my skillful mouth to satiate him. My hand wrapped around the base of his cock and I began sucking more earnestly, my motions practiced and eager as I flicked my grey eyes up at Victor.

It earned me some of the most satisfying male moans I could imagine. His pleasured noises so intensely deep and genuine, his voice so ripe with desire.

"Sis... Priscilla," he moaned out as I worked his shaft, and he helped guide my head. "Oh fuck... fuck you're so good at this," he grunted out, shuddering all over. "You're gonna make me pop if you keep this up..."

Those were magic words for me. I loved them, and

I felt that tingle in my pussy. For a moment, I felt like I wanted to just jump on my bed, have him defile me there. But this was about him. About convincing him that I was right here, that milking them dry and ruling over them was not as appealing as building a family of people who loved each other.

He was a sculpted adonis, every bit the perfect man in form. Albeit pale, but I liked that about him. He looked like a dangerous goth.

But through the subtle, sensual work of my tongue and mouth, I was making him putty in my hands. And he groaned, his knees trembling as he gasped out my name. And then... for the first time since we'd gotten carried away, and risked knocking me up... he blew his load into my mouth.

That thick load of creamy white seed flooded over my tongue, filling my mouth as he moaned loudly, his eyes rolled back, his head with it.

His taste was intoxicating, and I moaned as my knees quivered with desire. It had been so hard to resist the urge to fuck him raw, but I'd forgotten how much I loved making him cum in my mouth. I felt so powerful every time he did.

I didn't start sucking until he started twitching, and I eased off, cleaning the rest of his seed up with my tongue.

He shuddered all over, slowly coming back to his senses as I cleaned his cock of every last hint of his seed. And he looked down at me, with heavily lidded eyes.

"Fuck, sis... we had such a great plan... are you sure about this? And dammit, I should've pulled out of your mouth and dumped that load in your pussy. Just in case," he said with a sigh.

"Spend the day with me." I touched my fingers to my tingling lips, satisfaction written on my face. "There'll be plenty of other chances. And..." I stood up, still only at his chest, even in my high heels. "I think this is... I think we'll have an easier time keeping them under our control if we play nice and pool our resources."

The handsome black sheep of the Hawthorne family looked conflicted, but I could see that I was assuaging him. Making him more amenable to my idea for the family. A nice, satisfying climax down my throat helped a lot.

"It might not matter at all anyhow, Priss," he said with a sigh, pushing a hand back through his dark hair. "Grandfather was saying that he might end up leaving everything to uncle Arthur, since as the playboy of the family, he's never had to earn his way, not even like dad did by running the company."

I let out a little sigh of frustration.

"Grandfather seems like kind of a dick." I ran my hands over Victor's chest, kissing his pecs with affection. "I thought you were his favourite. And that you were the playboy of the family," I added on in jest.

He laughed at that wryly, looking at me as his strong hands slid to my hips, then around my waist.

"He might not have been fully serious. But hey... we gotta cover our bases, huh? Your little plan wouldn't go anywhere if you unite everyone... except the one guy who holds all the purse strings, would it?" he said, squeezing me in his arms against his hard chest, kissing me.

"Well, all you Hawthorne men are fucking kinky as hell. I don't know Arthur very well. He always just seemed..." I trailed off. It was hard to describe him. He was an enigma, in a way. He collected fine art, but never created anything himself. He just seemed to bounce around from New York to London to Beijing to Shanghai, returning back to some of the most expensive art known to man. He was always hosting lavish parties, but I'd only been to a couple. He didn't like kids around, and once I hit eighteen, he started inviting me, but by the time I'd arrived, he was nowhere to be found. Once, he even left his own party to head out on his private jet to some diplomat's estate instead.

So yea, I didn't know him well, and trying to figure out how to get him interested in me was going to be a challenge.

"Maybe I should arrange a 'meet cute'."

Victor arched a brow at me.

"A 'meet cute'?" he said, pausing his caressing, fondling hands as he stared. "What the fuck is that, sis?" he asked, sounding baffled.

"You know, like when the new girl goes into school and bumps into a guy and her books spill all over the floor, and the guy helps her pick them up, then they look in each other's eyes, and boom, love at first sight." I mulled it over for a second before adding on, "Or maybe a virgin auction. Though I bet they'd not take my word for that," I laughed.

Victor gave a groan as he cocked a half-smile and rolled his eyes.

"Not sure we're gonna be able to arrange a 'virgin auction' on such short notice anyhow. And it might strike uncle Arthur as odd if you lure him into a school you don't even go into just to bump into him," he said with a cheeky grin.

I flicked Victor's chest.

"I was just thinking of doing something to make him realize I'm not a little girl anymore. Come on, he's a playboy, I'm not going to be *just* another conquest.

That's not going to earn us an inheritance. I need to do something that makes him fall madly in love with me. Help me think," I said, tugging Victor to my bed and pushing him back onto it.

He was a lot bigger and stronger than me, but he played along and fell back atop the bed. His cock was still hard, and it bobbed with the motion as he looked up at me.

"Fuck sis, seducing guys is *your* speciality, *not mine*," he said. "Maybe just wear some... designer outfit that's fancy but sexy. Catch his eye with not only your body, but your keen sense of style," he remarked.

"See how smart you are when you're not teasing me?" I said as I moved onto the bed with him, my thighs wrapping around his. His cock throbbed against my mons and I smiled down at it. "God, you're still so hard. What a good little addict you are, big brother."

He groaned, his dark eyes sweeping over me, devouring me visually. He was so into me. But then... so far, all the Hawthorne men were. And his dick pulsed against my mound, as he slid his strong hands over my thighs, caressing them.

"I can't help it that you turned out to be such a perfect woman. In body and mind, sis," he said, before one hand wandered up to cup one of my tanned breasts.

I loved him feeling me up, exploring my body. And doing so in my bedroom was a special thrill. We'd always been careful to avoid each other's rooms. We didn't want to raise suspicion. But now the thought of getting caught was turning me on, and my pussy was dripping wet onto his thighs.

"Tell me more smart things."

He groaned, his hand squeezing and fondling my breast with the perfect amount of pressure. His cock pulsating with that insatiable need for me that made me feel so loved and needed by all the men of the family.

"Dammit sis, how am I suppose to think when you're draining all the blood from my brain to my dick?" he said with a wry grin.

"I want to fuck my uncle and make him fall in love with me, Victor. This is the best time for you to think about how I can get inside his mind," I reminded him, my hips rolling forward and back, teasing myself just as much as I was teasing him. I pushed my auburn hair over my shoulders, my high heels digging into my mattress. "What made you fall in love with me?"

He shivered at my teasing, and he looked up at me. And I saw the lust in his eyes but also... the love and adoration there. He held my hip and breast as he wet his lips.

"I fell in love with your charm and personality. How much more... real you were, than everyone else. How you could see the joy and value in things everyone else here rejects or ignores," he said, sounding so mushy and love.

I might act like a scheming temptress at times, but I was a romantic at heart.

My grey eyes scanned his face, a smile teasing at the corner of my lips.

"Mmm. You make me fall in love with you all over again when you look at me like that," I confessed. "How about we make love in my bed, huh? Like a real couple. Could even spoon for a while."

"That's what I've wanted all along, sis. What I was trying to let us have through this whole scheme," he said, that strong hand of his sinking into my soft yet supple breast. "I want you as my woman. My lover. My bride," he groaned before lifting me up and twisting me around so that we both lay side by side on the bed, him turning to me to kiss my shoulder and neck.

I pulled up the blankets over us as I curled my back into him, gathering my hair to the side so that it wasn't in his way.

"I feel like I can really be myself with you. Can explore my personality and who I am. It's just so... nice. You make me feel safe," I confessed to him. My ass found his cock, and I ground against him playfully. "You make me the woman I want to be."

He groaned as my bubbly round ass pressed back against his cock, and I felt it twitch and throb with desire as he wrapped his big strong arms around me. He held me close, and kissed my shoulder and neck as we spooned.

"I love all the parts of you I've seen, sis... from the parts that enjoyed my bad poems, to the part that apparently loves slutting it up with the entire family," he confessed in a throaty growl, right into my ear.

"Your poems are not bad," I chided him. My hands found his, resting atop him, encouraging him to touch and tease my body with his agile fingers. "And I do love slutting it up on your behalf. You awakened something naughty inside of me, Victor."

He moaned as our bodies ground together, and his hand found a breast again, to squeeze and mould it to the shape of his fingers. He groaned and shuddered, nibbling my earlobe as I felt him spurt pre-cum onto my backside.

"I really hope it's my child in you, sis..." he said, as his hand caressed my taut tummy. "Whatever happens, I'll treat it as if it's mine. But I really hope I got to claim you fully, in all ways, first."

"I hope so too," I admitted. "I want our child to

have your smarts, your depth, your dark edge. A little rebel." I shifted so that my ass was grinding against his abs, his cock slipping between my thighs and rubbing against my slick pussy lips. "Fuck, you're so huge, Victor."

He groaned deeply, and kept rubbing his dick along my slit, grinding our loins together so beautifully. It made my clit sing the way the head of his shaft rubbed over and past it, and he held me so tightly in his grasp.

"And your beauty, serenity, depth of charm and understanding... you have so much good in you, sis," he groaned, kissing me, trying to angle his hips just right for his cock to slip up into me again.

I wanted it, but more than that, I wanted to draw this moment out. To really luxuriate and enjoy it. It was the first time we'd had some privacy in a place comfortable enough to want to linger.

But, at my core, I was just as eager as him, and after a few unsuccessful jabs of his hips, I angled my pussy so that he could slip inside me. He was so hard, even though I'd just gotten him off in my mouth, and my cunny ached for him.

He gasped at the tight squeeze of my pussy, and I gasped with him, from the thick penetration of his cock. Because despite how much Hawthorne dick I'd taken in recent days, they always felt so big and filling, and I always felt so very grateful and whole to have them inside of me.

"F-Fuck sis," he grunted, his shaft throbbing in my wildly. He moaned and held himself in me real deep. "You can woo him... you can charm anyone," he told me, nuzzling into my neck, "just let your artsy side out. Show him your depth," he groaned as his hips began to tug back, to pump forward into me again.

I was glad that I'd locked the door, because I'm sure the moan I let out sounded half pained. It was my first time making love like this, and I was surprised by how perfectly his cock glided against the inner bundle of nerves. It was electric, and my thighs spread a little to let him push deeper into me.

"Oh God, Victor. We were made for each other."

His one hand gripped my hip tighter, holding onto me, keeping a good anchor on me as he dictated the pace of our love making. He pistoned his cock into me faster, harder, making me feel that deliciously long, thick shaft as it so satisfyingly struck my core.

"Fuck sis... we really were. We belong like this... as often as we can be," he moaned out.

There was nothing soft about our making love. Neither of us wanted that. We were a little soft hearted, and definitely in love, but when it came to sex, having it hard and dirty was the way we showed that love.

I grabbed onto the pillow for support, my pink canopy sheets filtering out some of the early afternoon light.

"I can't wait to take a pregnancy test and know that our baby is inside me!"

He shuddered and groaned, his towering, muscular form trembling from the pleasure my tight pussy brought him. It made me feel so powerful to be able to bring such gorgeous, powerful men to shuddering delight. To make them weak for me.

"Mmmph... not... not long now, sis. You'll be round with my baby in you. And everything will be so perfect," he grunted, caressing my skin, making me feel so worshipped, so appreciated and desired.

"I've wanted you for so long, Victor. I'm so glad we ended up together," I gasped. He was hitting my pussy just right, and it was starting to coil up, preparing for release. My toes were curling, my breasts rising and falling quickly against his wandering hands. I knew it wasn't going to be long, and I was going to be gushing all over him. But I wanted to hold out until he was ready.

But after blasting his load down my throat just moments before, he had a lot of stamina in him. Even in the face of the tight clench of my pussy, as my body sought to drain him dry. And so I got to listen to his pants and moans more, enjoy the way he held me as he made my bubbly ass ripple and quake with each pump.

Until finally, basking in the filtered light together, beneath the covers of my bed, I felt him begin to tense up. His cock stiffening extra hard, his breathing getting shallow as he shuddered.

"So... so close, sis," he grunted out.

"Cum in me, big brother," I told him in my throat-iest whisper. I needed it just as badly as I needed air, and I was perched on the edge of my own orgasm for so long I felt like I'd go mad if he didn't push me over the edge. My pussy tightened around him, taking him in so deep as I began to tremble.

His thrusts came on so deep and hard, so intense. It was such a satisfying end to our cuddling love-making, and I felt his shaft tense up, swell and... he gasped, grunted, and gave a choked cry. And then his cock began to erupt, shooting off more of his virile, Hawthorne seed deep inside of me, filling me up as my own body hit its limits.

I screamed, not holding anything back. I was completely unrestrained as pleasure crashed over me like the tide. His erratic thrusting, stabbing into me so deep, sent me reeling as my pussy vibrated around his throbbing dick.

"Yessss. Yes! I love you, Victor. Fuck I love you!"

His hands and arms squeezed around me, holding my breast and torso, almost crushing me to him as both our bodies exploded with such intensity. He shuddered and gasped, and we rode out our intense climaxes like that, screaming and moaning, filling my room with such lewd sounds.

"F-Fuck sis! I love you so fucking much!" He grunted as he spurt out his seed in such thick streams.

I was lost to pleasure. I'm not even sure if I didn't pass out or not. It was just so blissful, so much ecstasy coursing through my body, that I lost track of everything. Of everyone outside of the room, of the world beyond my bed. It was the moment you wish you could hold onto forever, and I was content to do just that when my phone began to ring.

I was so out of it, I just picked it up and answered it without even stopping to think that I was in a compromising position with my own brother. And that my brain was nearly fucked out of my skull.

"Hello?" I said, sounding a bit tired.

"Hey sweetie. It's daddy. Still catching up on lost sleep from our fun last night? You sound so tired," he said, his voice so smooth and caring.

"Oh, hey daddy." That kind of shook me out of it and made me realize that my brother's cock was still seeding my womb as we spoke. But... it was kind of hot, and I began idly grinding against Victor. "Yea, I feel like I'm fucked out of my mind right now. It was so good, though. Worth it," I said, teasing the two of them at once.

I couldn't see him, but I could feel Victor's own enjoyment of the messed up situation. I knew he was grinning as he fondled my breast, and resumed grinding his dick up in my pussy. My stiff nipple caught between two of his fingers.

"Mmm, why don't you go ahead and send me a picture once we're off the phone, huh?" he told me, and I could detect the desire in his voice.

"A picture? Yea, I can do that," I said with a devious grin. "I'm dripping wet just hearing you again."

"Ohhh baby girl, you have no idea how much I love to hear that," he said, and I'd never heard him sound so... enraptured and pleased on the phone. He meant what he said. "Wish I was calling just for fun, but is there a little favour you could do for me today, sweetie?"

"A favour? Oh, sure. I was just going to laze around my room for a while, but... anything for you,"

I said, my hand squeezing Victor's around my tit. It felt so huge in his palm, and for a moment I wondered if it was too early to feel the symptoms of pregnancy. When did a girl's tits grow anyways? Probably not this soon...

"Mmmm, that's my good little girl," father rumbled to me approvingly. "I'd forgotten that your uncle Arthur was coming today," he explained, "and there's no family member there ready to sign off on the delivery of some of his new stuff that's arriving before he is. Could you handle that? Have them take it over to Arthur's place. You know, the guest house, out back," he explained to me.

And all the while, Victor began to rock his hips, pumping his still turgid cock into me, teasing and taunting me with that delicious, slow motion.

I let out a little groan, and hoped it sounded like disappointment in the task rather than excitement at Victor's cock.

"Oh, sure Daddy. I'll make sure Uncle Arthur gets it, all wrapped up with a cute little bow," I managed out. "Where's the key for his house?"

"Mmm, knew I could count on you, my perfect little girl. You'll find the key up in my room, in my main office. It's in the desk, just check the top drawer on the left. Got it? Mmm, but don't forget to send me that picture before you get wrapped up in that work now, sweetie..."

"What kind of picture are you angling for? The light in here is amazing right now," I said, before thoughtfully adding, "my tits look huge."

I could hear him groan on the other end as he sat in the family's private plane.

"Show me those. And how wet you are for Daddy. I wanna see it all, sweetie. I miss you so bad, makes me wish I never left bed with you this morning," he confessed.

"My tits and pussy," I said with a little giggle, grinding against Victor's cock, with it still lodged firmly between my thighs. "I'll see what I can do. I've never taken a naughty picture before, so I hope it'll turn out alright."

Victor was making it harder and harder to hide the heat of my rising breathing, as his hips moved faster, pumping his dick into me. And he murmured into my ear quietly, so that Daddy couldn't make out what he said.

"You little slut... you just love having so much cock craving you," Victor murmured.

While on the other end of the line Daddy said, "Mmm, I know you'll look good no matter what, sweetie. You're the hottest girl in all the world. And

I've seen enough of the world to know that. So be a good girl for me, and I'll see you very soon, I hope."

"I'll be a good girl," I promised, already breaking the promise even as I said it. I had no intention of being a good girl. Victor was right. I was a slut at my core, and teasing the both of them was making me hornier than I'd ever been. "Can I play with myself for you... just for a few minutes? I want to hear your voice as I cum."

"Fuck you're bad," Victor murmured into one ear. As Daddy groaned into the other.

"Oh baby, how can Daddy say no to that, huh? I only wish I could be there, to dump another load into that perfect, tight pussy of yours while you cum on Daddy's cock," Father said.

I moaned, not having to hold back anymore. It was so fucking hot, and Victor obviously thought so too. He'd not even gotten soft, not for a second, even though he'd already cum in me twice. And I was wound up so tight I was losing my mind.

"Are you thinking of me in my little bikini? My pussy lips kissing the fabric?"

"Mmmm, fuck yes, sweetie. I need to see if there's a way to get you one even tinier while I'm away. I want you barely wearing anything but all the gold and jewelry that money can buy," he professed to me, while

Victor kept up his pleasing thrusts, his fondling touches. It was much better than masturbating myself, Victor handled the heavy lifting, while Daddy spoke to me so filthily.

I just had to lay there and take it.

The peak of luxury.

"God, it's like I can almost feel your big, thick cock thrusting into me, daddy. I'm on my side, in my bed, and I can feel your dick between my thighs. Thrusting up into my little pussy. I ache from last night, still, but you don't let up."

Of course, I didn't need to imagine it. Victor was doing it. And I got to hear my Father moan on the other end.

"Oh fuck sweetie, Daddy has to take his cock out and stroke it. Right here on the plane. Imagining being ball's deep inside of you again. Pounding that pretty little slice of perfection that's your pussy. I need to take you with me on the next flight, so you can ride me here instead," he groaned out.

"Ah, God, you're so big," I gasped, holding onto the bed as I trapped the phone between my head and the pillow. "I want your cum so bad I can't hardly stand it. I feel like I'll die without it!" I cried out, my pussy throbbing around Victor's cock.

Victor was doing his best to fuck me without

making too many loud clapping noises of his groin hitting my ass. But it was difficult. At least my moans and panting covered up those that he couldn't suppress.

"Oh fuck, baby. When Daddy gets back home, you'll be stuffed full of cum, drowning in it. I promise. I'll have so much to give you for being such a good little girl," he grunted, his own breathing heavier.

I felt filthy down to my very core.

That's probably what made me cum.

I was just completely losing myself in the game, in the ego that the Hawthorne men were stoking in me. I felt like a goddess, completely unstoppable, and I screamed as I came, my cunt trapping my brother's cock inside of me as my father was masturbating on the other end of the line.

And even though Victor had blown his load twice, something about the filthy scenario, and the irresistibly tight clench of my pussy did him in... again. And he gasped in my ear, as his whole powerful body tensed up, then began to shoot off a third load of his seed into me.

"Ohhh fuck baby, you sounded like you enjoyed Daddy's cock so much!" came my Father's voice from the other end of the phone. "Fuck, why'd I ever let you leave my side?"

I was whimpering and moaning too much to really answer him, my pleasure apparent in each and every panted breath I took. Moments passed as I tried to regain my sense of control, but even then, it was wavering.

"Oh God, Daddy, you're so good at fucking me. Even thousands of miles away."

He moaned on the other end. And Victor moaned into my ear. It was like having them both at once. And that was so intensely hot.

"Oh sweetie... you're too good to me. How was I ever supposed to resist the most stunning woman in the world? Say you'll come with me on my next trip, so we can have all manner of fun in the sky, in whatever corner of the world I end up traveling to. And all points in between," he begged.

"I'll come with you next time," I promised, coming down from my intense high. I was going to be so sore after this, but with how wet I was, it wasn't so bad. Hopefully. Because I had another Hawthorne man to wrap around my little finger, and I wasn't going to let a sore little pussy stand in my way. "I gotta go, Daddy, so I can get ready for Uncle Arthur."

"Mmmm, okay darling," he said with a great sigh. "Just remember to send me those pictures, huh? I'll need them to keep me company on this lonely, lonely flight," he said.

Of course, I had Victor holding me, massaging my breast, teasing me to want to make a squeak from the pinch of my nipple.

I resisted, though, much to his chagrin. He pinched me again and I gasped, speedily responding to father. "I will. Love you!" I clicked end on the call and tossed the phone back onto the nightstand. I turned my torso towards Victor, giving him a little flick on the shoulder.

"Oh you'd love Father to know that you got to me first, wouldn't you?"

He grinned at me so mischievously as I was left drooling his seed. And instead of responding right away, he leaned in and kissed my lips deeply, passionately. And we made out a while as he held me in his arms. As I softened and melted in his embrace, he slowly pulled back.

"Just couldn't help teasing my lil' sis," he said.

"I couldn't help being teased," I replied, my arms lightly around his neck. "But, apparently father set up a perfect ruse for me to be at Uncle Arthur's house when he returns home tonight. I'll ask the servants for a nice, light snack platter, as well as his favourite drink to be on hand. Dress like a ritzy artisté. Maybe become his muse," I mulled over in my mind. "But... I do find myself wishing that just for today, we could hide in here and just... play house."

Victor squeezed me to his hard chest and kissed me deeply again. We held each other, warmly making out and savouring the moment for as long as we could. Until finally he sighed as we disentangled.

"Better get those pictures to dad, and get ready for uncle Arthur I guess," he said. "Damn I can't wait for us to have more time and freedom to be together though, sis."

"I know. But... this is all for us. Building towards our future. It's worth it," I said as I lazily laid back on the bed. I wasn't quite sure my legs would work anymore, so I slowly dangled them over the mattress, my high heels grazing against the marble floor. "I wonder what Uncle Arthur has delivered today anyways."

"No fucking clue," said Victor with a sigh as he laid back on my bed, showing no intentions of getting up any time soon. But he looked absolutely gorgeous laying there, bathed in light, his rippling, sculpted physique on display like he belonged in some painting, or at least a stunning statue.

I stood on trembling legs, taking my time to steady myself as I grabbed my phone. I went to the side of the window where the light was bright but not harsh, and opened my photo app. I played with the angle and filters until I got my tits looking their best, then tried a more coy approach with my fingers between my thighs. I really didn't want father to see how full of cum I was, but I was in a hurry to obey.

I sent the best option for both off to father, then headed to the bathroom.

"God, I can't believe how much you can cum in one morning. You never cease to impress me, Victor."

"Well what can I say, sis?" he remarked with a cocky grin from the other room. "You make for an amazing muse," he said with a low chuckle. "Pure inspiration, that body and charm of yours."

It didn't take long for the messages from Father to start coming in too:

"Fuck I am going to lose my mind thinking of how hot you are, and how foolish I was to leave you at home."

"Mmm damn, that's gorgeous."

Then:

"Fuck, you still have my cum inside you? I see some of it dribbling out in that last pic."

Oops.

"Mhm. Barely opened my legs at all this morning. I

didn't want to waste a drop," I texted back, giggling as I started running the bath.

"Whoops, got some of your cum in that last pic. I didn't notice it, but dad did," I said to Victor. "Get in here and help me get cleaned up. I gotta look perfect for my date with our dear ol' Uncle Arthur."

Victor groaned as if I had asked him to perform a tedious chore for me. But the way he got in there almost immediately, with a grin on his face, told me he was more than eager.

"Careful sis. We might end up going a fourth time, and you'll be too worn out for uncle Arthur to take a crack at your pussy," he teased as he came in, to help bathe me, and prepare for our evening ahead.

We were able to resist going at it again, but we were anything but chaste. By the time I was dressed, Victor was raging hard again and begging to jerk off. I let him watch me as I pulled on my short, cream, designer lace dress. It dipped low between my breasts, and the tulip skirt edged up along my left thigh. The fabric was almost translucent, and even though it looked high class, it also looked slutty as hell.

I pulled on a long strand of pearls, wrapping it around my neck twice, and grabbed a couple matching bracelets as well. I dried my hair, fluffing it up to make it look full and slightly wavy, using some sea salt spray to give it that wild, untamed look.

"What do you think?" I asked Victor in the mirror, watching him as he stroked his cock to the sight of me. "Should I wear my fuck-me pumps or be a bit more casual and grab a pair of kitten heels?"

His hand slid up and down the length of his manhood as he sized me up. And he didn't pause as he licked his lips then responded as thoughtfully as he could, under the circumstances.

"Looks great. Do the fuck-me pumps, it'll contrast the more classic lace real nice," he said, as a bead of pre-cum formed at the head of his shaft.

I went over to my closet, bending at my waist so that the skirt rose up high on my ass, showing off the crease where it met my thighs. I found a pair of cream heels, and put them on, doing a little twirl for Victor.

"What do you think? He gets a visit from his very grown up, wild and mischievous niece who's just begging to be his muse," I purred with a dreamy smile.

Victor was my enraptured audience, and he missed not a split-second of my little display. He groaned and bit his lower lip as he nodded to me.

"Fuck, that's perfect sis. You'll have him as putty in your hands in no time," he remarked, though he hadn't for one moment stopped stroking his shaft as he watched me.

I went to him, strutting forward in my heels, my fingers going in on either side of my breasts and lightly tugging open the dress. I squeezed my tits out of the fabric, letting them bounce free, pressed together with just the pearls between them.

"You can finish if you're going to be quick, but otherwise I have to go," I said, offering him one of my breasts to suckle or fondle. "Just don't get anything on me."

His eyes were glued to my exposed tits right away, and as I came to him he put one of his strong arms around me. His hand cupped my ass as he bent down from his great height, to kiss and lick around my nipple.

"Fuck sis... I'll hurry," he grunted, spurting some pre-cum before he wrapped his lips around my teat and began to suckle as his hand pumped his shaft fast and hard, workin up and down that veiny, pulsating girth.

I felt so powerful in that moment. Like a Queen, receiving a special gift from her most devoted subject. My nipple instantly hardened in his mouth, excited by that perfect pressure, the exquisite whip of his tongue.

I stroked the back of his head, encouraging him as I felt that tingle of wetness grow between my thighs.

I wanted to do more than just watch his strong hand stroke off his cock, but I knew I had to save myself for uncle Arthur. Who knew how it would go with him, and it wouldn't do to show up already overly sore and exhausted.

So instead I listened to Victor's moans, felt the way his tongue swirled around my nipple, and then watched as his thick cock erupted. Long, pearly white strands of cum blasting out of his cock like lewd little ropes, as he groaned against my tit, making it hum and vibrate.

He was very careful not to spill a drop on me, and I cooed in appreciation to him.

"Good boy."

I pet his hair, letting him slowly come down from his high before I took a step back, squeezing my tits back into the dress. "Now, wish me luck in seducing our uncle."

Eight

ictor was panting, his broad, muscular chest heaving as his hand still lay at his cock, even after he'd drained the last drop onto my floor. He looked at me with forbidden yearning as I tidied myself up, but licked his lips and nodded.

"Good-luck sis. It's all depending on you now," he said, running his free hand back through his dark hair as he gazed at me longingly.

"Love you," I said as I practically skipped to the door, down to the massive foyer. The estate was large. Like... it took me ten minutes to get to the front door after going to Father's room to grab the key, but then I realized that a delivery would probably go to the servant's entrance, and it took me a little longer to figure out where that was. I never had reason to go there before. But tucked in the East wing, in the rear, I finally found a spacious entryway with tactful decorations. It seemed like the servants made this place their own, since it didn't have my father's taste.

"Milly?" I called out, trying to find my favourite servant. She was around my age, maybe a little older... or younger, it was hard to say. Her mother was a servant, as was her grandmother, so Milly was a natural at the job. It didn't surprise me when I heard her singsong voice ring out from up the stairs.

"Miss Priscilla? Whatever are you doing back here?" She met me at the bottom of the stairs, her uniform freshly pressed, her light brown hair in a simple bun. She was a plain looking woman, but with some mascara and a bright red lipstick, she'd definitely turn heads.

"Uncle Arthur has some packages coming, and Father asked me to see to it."

"Mr. Hawthorne? Oh. Well, yes, some of your Uncles boxes have arrived, they're bringing the rest in."

"Could you have them bring it to the guest house? I have the key, and then we can get it all set up for him. Give him a little surprise."

Milly didn't look so convinced, but she knew better than to question a Hawthorne, even if it would potentially put her in conflict with another Hawthorne.

"Of course, Miss. We'll need you to sign for it anyways. I can't find your brothers at all."

"Don't worry about them, today," I said with a smile, touching my index finger to her chin, tipping it up slightly. "Today, your primary duty is to help me make sure that when Uncle Arthur returns back, he feels welcomed. Will you see to it that a tray with his favourite pastries is prepared for his arrival? Along with a bottle or two of whatever it is he drinks."

"Of course, Miss Priscilla. I'll see to it right away."

And like that, I began setting the staff to a frenzy of activity. First it was Milly, but then soon it was nearly all of them. They were rushing around, taking the crates over to the guest house across the lush lawn and cobblestone walkways.

The "guest house" that was uncle Arthur's residence, was a mansion all it's own by any normal human standards. And I had the servants cracking open the crates, to eye the paintings, sculptures, rugs and tapestries that came out of them.

Luckily my own expertise with fashion and design paid off, and I instantly knew where most of it should go to complement the existing art. And one piece in particular, a gorgeous statue of a sailor and a mermaid, in the nude, demanded to be held in some central point of prestige. And I practically rearranged the upstairs level of the main hall in its entirety, to make room for it where the stained glass windows--that uncle Arthur had taken from some nearly ancient church in France, and installed in the manor--coalesced into a beautiful pattern of light upon the stonework.

I was feeling pretty pleased with myself, and since I wasn't having to do the manual labour of lifting up massive statues and art all day, I was feeling rejuvenated by the time I heard one of the servants call out.

"Mister Hawthorne, welcome back!" There was a little tremor of fear in his voice, to be caught in his house, and I knew I had to make my entrance.

I walked to the grand staircase, and began my descent. Each long leg in front of the other, my heels carrying me with grace and dignity as my tits bounced with each step.

"Uncle Arthur," I smiled, warm and relaxed, as if it wasn't at all unusual for me to have been in his house without his being there. "Father tasked me with delivering your packages, but I've been very mischievous about it. I couldn't resist taking a peek. And you know what they say about Pandora's Box."

Uncle Arthur looked like no other Hawthorne in

how he dressed and styled himself. His hair was chin length, wavy, he had the look of a hairy bohemian about him as he stood in his loose linen shirt, with the beaded embroidery around it. It was probably from some exotic far south country, judging by the look of it.

And his skin was so beautifully tanned. He was the only member of the family that seemed to enjoy the sun as much as I did. And as his dark eyes swept around the foyer he studied my handiwork with his scrutinizing gaze. I could see he was quite serious.

"You're quite the precocious young girl, Priscilla," he said, before his dark gaze landed on me, and he did a bit of a double take. "Sorry, quite a precocious young lady," he said with a half-cocked smile as he observed me for the first time in ages. "My goodness, you have not only developed a keen sense of style, you've truly come into yourself," he said as he opened his arms to me.

I went to him, though my arms didn't go about his waist like a child. They went around his neck, my firm tits pressing to his abs.

"I haven't seen you in years. I never intended to neglect you, Uncle. And seeing your taste, that's all the more true. I think you and I have much in common." My arms still wrapped about his neck, I pulled back a little to look at his handsome face. "Spend the day with me?"

While I'd gotten his attention with my appearance at first, Arthur showed himself surprisingly resilient for a Hawthorne man as he wrapped his arms around me, and embraced me. He didn't let his gaze dip to my breasts as all the others had. He held his casual, confident charm as he smiled at me.

"How can an uncle say no to such a proposition, huh?" he remarked, before glancing around the place. "And maybe you can tell me a bit about your method. And I'll be intrigued to know what prompted you to place things where you did," he said with a grin.

I perked up, delighted that, at least, my talents interested him.

"Sure. Milly, I think we're all done for the day, other than the--" I was going to say the pastries when I noticed the servant carrying them in and discreetly setting them in the spacious living room. "And the--" I was cut off again by Milly motioning to the bar area, where two glasses and a bottle of aged Moroccan wine. I smiled at her, affection pouring out of me. She really was on top of it. I didn't need to doubt her at all.

"Thank you, Milly. That's everything for the day. Please have all who helped here today prepare a special meal for yourselves tonight. You've earned it."

"Thank you, ma'am," Milly said, giving me a curtsey before heading off with the other servants.

Uncle Arthur and I disentangled, and he headed over towards the large side-room, where the living room and bar awaited us. He went to the bottle of wine, and immediately began to inspect it.

"A grey wine. My, you do have exotic tastes in more than just fashion," he said to me with a half-crooked smile, before he began to twist out the cork. "I suppose you're old enough for a nice glass of wine with your dear old uncle now, aren't you?" he said, with a loud pop to accentuate the statement as the cork was pulled free.

"Father's been allowing me wine on Christmas for years. I'd be happy to join you," I said as I walked to his side. "Where were you in the world this time that you amassed such a wealth of fabulous art?"

He poured up the lightly hued wine with a practiced hand, filling both glasses up to the midway point in a smooth pour before setting the bottle aside and offering me a glass. He lifted his own, taking his time to smell the aroma of the wine.

"A truly excellent choice, Priscilla," he said with a smile, and without drinking any yet, he leaned against the bar and looked to me. "I was doing a bit of a jaunt around the world. Following my fancies to South

America, then Africa, across south-Asia. Spent some time in the Himalayas, before a detour to the Australian desert. And then... a nice cruise along the Antarctic before a final stop in Central America. Then home," he explained with a smile. "It takes a lot of exploration to find the right pieces. And inspiration."

"That sounds like a very exhausting journey," I said with a laugh. "But clearly, it was well worth it, considering the pieces that you've brought back. You have a keen eye for rare talents. Things easily overlooked by lesser men." I raised my glass to him. "To finding inspiration in unlikely places, and keeping an open mind," I toasted.

He looked to me, inscrutable as he was. And seemed to stare into my soul, before cracking a smile and raising his glass to clink against mine softly.

"To inspiration and an open mind," he said with a warmth that was new and interesting at least, before sipping the wine. He licked his lips and remarked, "That is truly an exquisite choice. Well done, Priscilla."

"I know we haven't spent much time together, but I knew that you were a man of fabulous taste. That narrowed down the selection nicely. And France or Portugal seemed too obvious, too common. But... Morocco, that's surprising. You have all of the taste, with the peculiarities and excitement that you can only find once you look outside of the conventional."

He smiled, but my flattery didn't seem to impress him as he turned towards the platter of pastries.

"Well, you really have laid out the welcome mat for me. I can't recall ever returning from a sojourn to so pleasant a welcome," he said, before taking up one of the tiny little puffy pastries, taking a moment to help himself to one. "Mmmm, perfect. The staff here always gets them just right."

He was going to be a tough nut to crack, but I didn't let disappointment enter my mind. I just had to find the right angle to work him on.

"They do. They were most helpful to me today, helping get this all set up for you." It was the truth, and maybe he saw himself as an every-man, a wealthy bachelor of the people. "I just told them where things needed to be placed, to bring out the beauty in each piece."

He savoured that single puff pastry, before washing it down with the wine.

"Ah, those two are paired *very* well, Priscilla," he said to me, using his thumb to clear the corners of his mouth in case any cream from the pastry remained. But it didn't, he'd ate it without a single bit of mess. "Tell me, why haven't you gone on more travels yourself, hm? You're clearly old and mature enough for it now," he said, turning half-way towards me.

"I've not thought about it much. I just always felt fulfilled here. But you do bring up some excitement in me that's fresh and interesting," I mused, taking a pastry and teasing my tongue along the top, scooping up some of the whipped cream from the berries. "Where would you take me if we were to travel together?"

He eyed me, clearly not missing any of my little show, but he betrayed nothing about any effect it had on him. If any. He just sipped some more wine and then said:

"Oh, that's easy. Carcosa," he said with a smile. "I plan to make a sojourn there myself, on my next journey out. Of course, I need to finish up studying my new finds, and getting a full appreciation for them first. It wouldn't do to head to a place like lost Carcosa without being fully prepared."

I raised a brow.

"We'd travel to a lost city together?" My smile grew a little bit devious, "Oh, don't tell me you want to run away with me to never be heard of again. No wonder you're the bad boy of the family."

He cracked a grin at me, looking quite amused by my banter.

"Oh, ideally we'd be heard of again. Quite prominently. There are countless places in this world to see. But the best would be the ones not intended to be seen, I'd say. Wouldn't you?" he asked, as he sipped some more wine. "I've been working on putting together bits of info. Little tidbits of information, to find it. Art is magnificent in and of itself, of course, but it led to my little obsession in finding the lost city. In doing something no other has done in ages."

"I do like the sound of that. Or maybe it's just the way you put it. You have a way to excite places in me that I didn't know existed. Being the first to explore something... Well. I suppose first to explore it in a long while, considering it's a city, so someone had to explore it at some point." I mulled that over as I put a pastry in my mouth, daintily chewing it. A crumb got stuck to my lip gloss, but I resisted the urge to lick it away.

He was slow and methodical about his actions and words, and he looked at me a moment. Then slowly reached up to gently wipe the corner of my lips, clearing it of the pastries remains with his thumb.

"Precisely. The first in a very, very long time," he said with a smile, before he brought his thumb to his face and placed it in his mouth, suckling it clean as he then casually looked to me, then away before sipping some more wine.

I stared at him, my grey eyes the colour of our wine, my long lashes wrapped in black mascara to make the contrast even more notable.

The corner of my lips curved upwards as I met his rich, honey-brown gaze.

"How's it taste?"

"Delightful," he said with such casual confidence. He didn't smile, didn't play it off as anything. He just reacted so casually calm and in control as he took up the wine bottle and topped up our glasses again. "I plan to stick around a while this time. As long as it takes to pore over my findings, and figure out my next trip. Could be months, maybe years," he said.

My lip twitched in amusement.

"Feels like the longest you've been home before this has been a day or a week. Just long enough to throw a party and leave me chatting with all your oldest friends, unable to even catch your eye."

He pushed a hand back through his long, wavy hair and smiled at me lightly.

"No reason things have to go that way this time, is there? We'll have lots of time to hang out, get to know one another now. Come on, show me where you put the pieces. I want to know why," he said, as he led the way back out into the foyer.

As we walked, I described why I moved things and

arranged the art as I did. I had to make room for some of the new pieces, so had changed things up pretty drastically in the few hours I had full reign of his house. Brighter pieces were moved into the living areas, to lighten up the room and add some colour to spaces that had been mostly monochromatic. He had a lot of colourful tapestries and rugs from all over the world, so I spent some time matching themes, arranging things to be in flattering and complimentary positions. His living room was primarily Europe, greys and blacks and whites begging for a little splash of the Mediterranean. His entry way demanded joviality and a strong sense of personality, so I matched it off of what I remembered of Uncle Arthur's eclectic taste, bringing in reds and navy to give the room energy and motion, a sense of being transported into an exotic land.

"The upstairs is where I put the old world charm, though. I wanted it to feel more classic, more eternal. I thought the light of the stained glass, when the morning light hits it, should bathe the sailor and mermaid in its shimmering glow, making it feel as if shore is so near by, yet... unreachable. They're lost to their fates, and embrace the beauty, even if it means that everything they've ever known would disappear over the horizon."

He listened without much commentary, just

following along beside me, thoughtfully nodding at times, ever studying the art and my placement of it. Until finally we were standing in front of the sensual statue of the mermaid and sailor, and he was studying it in the cascade of colourful, brilliant light.

"You really have done well," he remarked, wetting his lips as he studied the large statue, with it's stunning curves carved by someone who was clearly a master craftsman. "It's quite striking in the colourful rays... almost as if you're seeing it under water, in the brilliant lights beneath the sea from whence it last rested," he remarked, lifting his head and smiling towards me.

I smiled back at him.

"That's what I was hoping the effect would be. I had to move a lot of things to make room for it, and though the servants wouldn't complain, I know it's... heavy. So I'm relieved to hear that you think it's an appropriate space for it." I looked at the statue, over the mermaid's body, up towards her bared breasts.

"She's beautiful."

"No more so than you, which is to say... quite beautiful indeed," he remarked as he walked around the statue, sipped his wine, then smiled back at me. "Well done, Priscilla. You've not only made this a very pleasurable homecoming, but... you saved me a lot of work too. Work I don't normally mind, of course. But it's nice to be able to share my fascination and fancy with *someone* in this family, for once."

"Perhaps the Hawthorne Estate needs more beauty and wonder in its halls. Father and Malcolm are too busy with their own pursuits, of course, and Victor prefers the written word to physical works of art, but... I think they'd all appreciate it, so long as it was presented in an appealing way."

It was all honest, but I had no idea how close I was to having him break through the boundaries of the taboo. To take a forbidden chance. At times I felt like it was so near, so possible, and then he'd become professional and casual once more. I recognized the strategy, though.

It was what I did to Malcolm.

Tugged him along. Reeled him in, then let the line grow slack, until the fish was begging to be caught.

I licked my lips at the realization.

"I didn't do much in your bedroom, though. I wasn't sure what to do in there. What type of vibe you wanted to go for. After all, you've mostly been entertaining in that room, more than sleeping, I expect."

He smiled at me, a certain knowing look, before he gestured down the hall towards his room.

"Come, we'll discuss it a bit," he said, as he led me

on down, to the big double-doors that opened to his bedroom.

That massive space with it's grand, two-story tall windows, thick crimson drapes, the old bookshelves up on the second floor. While down below were the posh sofas. And his bed in the centre, circular and ridiculously lavish. Draped in silks and fine cushions.

And all around the edges of the room, were strange and exotic pieces of art from around the world. Things even I had no idea what to make of, even as he showed me a few, telling me of where they came from, mostly places I didn't recognize.

"It's all the finest works I could find. Each having its own distinct personality," he said, and I felt that. It was like some of the statuettes and statues with eyes were watching us as we went around the room.

"This is not at all what I expected," I said, inspecting one of the images, a wild looking woman carved of some ebon stone. "And yet, it fits you to a tee." I felt so out of place in the room. It was my first time seeing it, and it felt like something out of a movie. It just had a different air about it.

It was like everything was arranged to make the bed the centre of things, so that the art could be enjoyed from all angles around while he lay there and rested.

And he sipped his wine as I commented, before smiling back at me.

"You think so?" he asked, a brow raised. "It's a pleasing little sanctuary, I gotta give it that. Something I'm more than pleased to return to after a long voyage, I'll confess," he remarked, one hand in his tight pants back pocket, as he strolled around the bed, sizing up the art in the light that streamed through the towering windows. It helped draw attention to his round, firm ass.

He was so different from the others, but he still had Hawthorne blood in him. That meant he was tall, fit, and irresistible.

We were toying with each other, though, and I wondered which of us would win.

Which of us should win.

"How many people have you had up in this sanctuary, Uncle?"

He cracked an amused smile, and he peered back at me over his shoulder.

"Jealousy doesn't become you, sweet niece," he remarked before sipping some more wine and rounding about the bed to come towards me again. "What if I told you: many, and yet not as many as you might expect. So few appreciate the work here, after all.

But... I thought you might begin to," he said with a smile.

"I'm not jealous," I said with a little pout, my gaze upon him like a scolded child. "I'm simply... curious. You have an eclectic taste. I'd like to learn more."

He seemed to find that amusing, and he came to me. His hand cupping my jawline, as his thumb caressed my cheek.

"You've got a real passion for my art collection, is that it, dear niece?" he asked me, his voice smooth and yet rich. So syrupy and seductive. He undoubtedly had any woman he wanted in his travels.

Even I felt like a little minnow, trying to swim in his pond. Even the idea of him devouring me seemed an acceptable outcome to having him notice me.

"I'm full of passion," I murmured, as if I were in a trance. I was letting myself be stripped bare of my ego and cunning. Letting him see the sweet, needy thing underneath.

His thumb was smooth as it slid over my skin, caressing me. Making me tingle with anticipation and rising eagerness.

"There is one other find I've brought back, that might interest you," he said with a wry smile, before heading over to his travel satchel, which one of the servants must've taken from him and ran on ahead to his room. But as he opened it up, he paused and looked back at me. "That is if you're sure you have the passion enough to dare it... I will, after all, insist on seeing it upon you."

"The only thing that rivals my passion is my curiosity," I said, taking a few steps towards him. My legs felt a little like jelly, and I was getting antsy. It was different with the others. I felt secure that, by the end of the night, they would be mine.

But I was worried that my Uncle was all teasing, no pleasing.

He looked amused with my response, then resumed opening up his satchel.

"It was the garb of a high priestess, in some long lost realm. I found word of it from a sailor in Kingsport, but it eventually took me to the other side of the world. To the ruins of an island nation that was wiped out of existence about two centuries ago," he explained to me before taking out the gauzy fabric of the gown. It would be see-through to wear.

And after that, he took out the most fascinatingly gleaming gold and gemmed jewelry. Bracelets, anklets, belts, and then, at the very bottom, wrapped in so much silk... he took out and unveiled the final piece.

"This is the absolute pinnacle. The sacred tiara of the high priestess herself," he said, unveiling the gleaming, unique thing, clearly intended for a petite lady's brow.

My lips were parted, and it felt... poignant.

Sacred.

I stared at each piece, closing the distance between us as I inspected it.

"Uncle... This is phenomenal. Beautiful. Ethereal," I said, not yet touching any of it. Father brought me back jewels that could buy mansions in some places, but this was absolutely priceless.

Irreplaceable.

He stared at the final piece itself, and the unique gemstone at the peak of it.

"The trapezohedron gemstone here, is singularly unique," he remarked before turning to me, the tiara held aloft. "Would you like to try it on?" he asked, a curious smirk teasing the corners of his lips.

"I'm not one to break a promise," I said before biting on my lower lip. My clear, grey eyes scanned his face. "I just don't want to ruin it. It looks so delicate."

His grin grew at that, and he looked me up and down.

"Don't worry. It's still made of gold metal. You won't harm it," he said, reaching up to very delicately slide the tiara into place atop the crown of my head. He took a step back and admired it, licking his lips.

"You have to put on the rest of it too. The ensemble must be completed," he said, sounding so intense.

I stared at him, confused by his reaction. It didn't seem like this was all just a ploy to get me undressed, somehow. All the same, it seemed that we were headed in that direction, and my fingers wrapped around the ends of the lace belt, lightly tugging it so that the dress fell open in the middle. My cleavage was released, my wet pussy politely tucked between my legs, my tanned skin gleaming in the filtered light of his room.

This time he looked. His eyes sweeping over my body, observing my perky, bare breasts, the light glistening between my thighs. He didn't comment, didn't smirk, didn't do much of anything except study and appreciate me for what I was.

"Good," he said at last, caressing his trimmed, dark beard. "You've the perfect size and shape for it," he remarked, letting his eyes move to the assembled items that made up the priestesses' ancient garb.

I shrugged off the dress, turning to place it on the edge of his bed. I wanted him to see my legs, shapely and toned, before I took off my heels. My ass was firm, and I ran a finger idly over it before I turned to face him again, stripping away my pearl jewellery.

"I'd feel more comfortable if you put it on me, Uncle."

He didn't balk or smirk at that, he just went to the bed beside me. He picked up the gauzy dress with care, then began to drape it over me. The fabric felt light as air, and he wound it about me, covering my breasts, my loins, yet leaving neither anything but fully exposed. The fabric was, after all, perfectly see-through. And it draped down over my long, shapely legs.

And after that, he began to take up the ritual gold vestments, the large necklace that made up for the absence of weight in the cloth, by feeling like a great heft around my neck. And he took my hair, freeing it before he attached the rest, bit by bit. He treated me like I was part of his art exhibit.

"There," he said at last, taking a step back.

I stood as still as a statue, watching him so intently. It was so strange. Yet I couldn't deny that it had an erotic appeal, all on its own. My nipples were stiff and my pussy was oh so wet, so needy. But still I stood there, staring at him.

"So what am I a priestess of?"

"Impossible to say, precisely," he said, walking around me, studying me like I was another of his works of art. "But beauty and fertility are obvious guesses," he said, "and you fit the role perfectly. Now that you're of age. I doubt anyone could emanate such qualities more thoroughly than you right now, Priscilla."

I turned my head to look at him, a small smirk on my lips.

"I don't think most uncles talk about their niece's fertility with such... interest." I didn't shrink from his view. I even puffed up a little, feeling some of my ego wrap around me like a protective cocoon once more.

He cracked a slight little smile at that, seeming undaunted by my sudden turning of the tables. He just stroked his beard and studied me.

"It's simply impossible to ignore. And just the truth," he remarked. "I'll have to get a painter to capture you in this sometime. You look more exquisite in it than I dared dream," he remarked so confidently. Just awed a bit by the artistic splendour... and a hint of his own arousal.

"So... is this all serendipity?" I asked as I stepped towards him. "That you find your sweet little niece, all grown up, all nice and ripe, and show her a present you bought for her on your travels?" I was practically purring, my hand finding his bare chest, fingers running through the thick hair.

He watched me, his dark eyes so unreadable. But he laughed a little at that.

"No offence, dear niece. But I didn't 'buy' it, and

I'm not giving it to you... not quite," he said with a faint grin on his face. "But I do enjoy seeing it on you. You capture the image of that seductress high priestess... perfectly," he remarked, reaching a hand out, to lightly trail just his index finger along my hip, my waist. Only the gauzy fabric between us, but it felt like it was not there at all.

My eyes fluttered at the touch.

"You've no problem taking what you wish, without regard for taboos, is that it?"

"And neither do you, it seems," he remarked with intense amusement at my behaviour. He licked his lips as his hand came to cup my breast, his thumb teasing around the edge of my areola. "Art is ritual. True art, that is," he explained, "and this all makes for the most exquisite of rituals... of course, if we go about it the right way. As the ritual was intended," he said so cryptically, a glint of desire in his eyes.

"You tell me what to do and I obey, is that it?" I asked with a laugh. He was being so mysterious, but I just figured he was into BDSM or something. I had no issue playing the role of the naughty priestess, if that's what it took to bind him to me.

Hell, I knew I'd enjoy it.

"You'll find I can be very obedient, when I want to be."

He laughed at that, as his other hand came up and slid around to caress the swell of my bubbly, round ass. He squeezed it, sinking his fingers into that flesh before licking his lips.

"A priestess of beauty and fertility, for starters... can't go about the business of carnality, with anything but raw abandon," he said in his delicious voice.

Oh God.

He knew how to talk to a woman, that much was for real.

I was blushing from head to toe, my breathing catching in my throat as I stared at him, felt his hands on my body. It was so wrong, and that made it even more delightful. More exciting.

"That won't be a problem."

"Good," he said with a faint smile, as his hand at my ass slipped downwards, his fingers curling inwards between the two gauzy straps of fabric. So that two of his digits slid along my slit, caressing it, feeling it's glistening, ripe wetness. He fingered me for a moment, masterfully, teasingly. Then plucked his digits away, to inhale my scent, to taste my honey with a lick.

"Mmm, you're quite ready. I can see that much. I trust you're not on the pill or anything..." he said with a cocky grin.

"I'm not on the pill, Uncle Arthur," I said, my

own cocky grin a shadow of itself. I was losing my mind with how he was teasing me. Unlike with Father and Malcolm, I felt totally out of control, at the mercy of someone else's desires and wishes, and I hated how much it turned me on.

My hands explored his chest as I looked up at him.

"What else do we need to do for this little ritual of bedding your niece?"

"Good. That would ruin everything if you were," he said, before smearing some of the remaining honey from my slit onto my lips. And then he leaned in and kissed it away, his tongue traveling over my own glossy morsels, before his tongue delved inside my mouth. And we made out like that, slow but sensual and passionate for a long time. His arm coiling back around me, his fingers finding my eager, ready slit again, fingering it, pumping his digits in and out as we made out. Until I was about ready to explode, and it was then his lips left mine.

"I need you to be honest with me. In words, yes. But most importantly in deed and desire," he husked, sounding like a guru more than my artsy uncle.

I didn't want to say a single thing that would make him resist me now. I was wrapped around his finger, not the other way around, and my body was seeking out his with such raw need. My hand dipped down from his chest until it was wrapped around the outline of his shaft, and I began rubbing it with my palm.

"Like this?"

"That's your truth," he said to me so simply, but in the face of his calm I could feel how stiff he'd become. I could feel the pulse of its desire rising as I touched his manhood. "You crave your uncle's cock. And the gift it promises to give you. You'll make a most stunning priestess of fertility, once you're round and swollen with my seed," he said so brazenly, before kissing me again, passionately. The taste of my own honey lingering between our tongues as we made out.

Fuck! He was so hot.

My hand rubbed him eagerly, my other arm tossed around his neck as my body ground against his. I was like a wild and untamed thing. He was absolutely right. That was what I wanted. The estate, well, that was all just a bonus. I wanted it, because Victor wanted it. But he'd unleashed me upon the family, and in doing so, helped me find my calling.

My mouth pressed against his, tongue teasing his lips.

We had fast went from a detached, artistic approach to our flirtations, to an outright madly passionate one. And my tall, striking uncle was groping and fondling me, holding me so tightly as he picked me up, one hand on my ass--with fingers buried in my cunt--and the other on my thigh. He took me to the bed, and laid me back upon it as he got up over me on his knees.

"We'll enact an ancient fertility rite not practiced in centuries. It'll be something for us both to remember, despite how much we've both clearly enjoyed the act before now," he said, with such a look in his eyes. That knowing glint making it seem as if he saw right through me, to all my schemes and shenanigans. My coy games and flirtations.

It was intense, but I didn't shrink from it. I couldn't, even if I wanted to. I was ensnared, my hips undulating in time to his rhythm, helping him finger my soaking wet pussy.

"What do I have to do?" I asked, my legs spread as I stared up at him. My breasts were heaving with each frantic breath, my lips parted and glossy from our kisses.

He pulled his fingers from my slit again, smeared the honey over his tongue before licking them clean. Then he began to unbuckle his belt, opening up his trousers. And he spoke as that thick, Hawthorne cock spilled forth. And I got to see that of all the Hawthorne men, he had the most unique of members. The brothers and their father were all nearly identical, but uncle Arthur's dick had a little extra rigidity to his bulbous crown, that promised a special little sensation.

"Open up to your truth, sweet Priscilla," he said, as he tugged his pants down to let his heavy balls spill out. "That's all you need do. Because you're already every bit the slut that the role of high priestess calls for, no?"

I smiled, taking it for the compliment it was, as my hand was already reaching out for his cock. It wasn't even a conscious pull. He was right, my desires were... ignited.

"You say the hottest things," I murmured as my fingers wrapped around his dick with such a sense of appreciation. My thumb pulled forth some of his precum, wettening his helm with it. "And what truth are you opening yourself up to, dear Uncle?"

He reached up and caressed my cheek so softly, so fondly. All while his dick pulsated wildly in my dainty grasp. And he smiled down at me, desire kindled in his eyes as he pulled his top off, tossing it aside to loom over me, his bare, hairy chest with a nice amount of muscle to it. And tanned through perfectly. It was clear he hadn't been wearing that shirt a lot in the hotter areas of the world.

"My truth is that I live for the experience of artistry. And you are pure artistry, my sweet little Priscilla," he said with a hint of a lusty growl, before he bent down. His hand lightly pushed aside the gauzy fabric as his mouth sealed around my teat and he suckled, while his cock was thrust along my slit, causing it to glance over my clit.

I gasped as he sucked my tit, his cock so teasingly close to my wet, wanting cunt. It was actually annoying how wet I was, because if I wasn't, maybe he'd not have glided right past my slit. I tried to angle him, but he was the one in control, and every time I tried to spear myself on him, he would readjust, teasing me to impossible heights of desire.

"God... Just... Fuck me," I pleaded, so pent up I felt like I might explode if I didn't get his dick in me right away.

But he wouldn't give me what I wanted, not right away. He tugged at my teat, licked at my nipple, until finally he let it snap back to my chest with a jiggle. And he grinned at me, kissing his way up my collarbone, to my neck. Where he nibbled at me, before his voice came husky and deep into my ear.

"You smell so deliciously fertile... so ripe for the seeding. Mmm, you think it's all decided, but... I know it's not," he husked cryptically into my ear, and before I could ask him anything more about it... he thrust his dick up inside me with one sharp push, impaling me hard and fast. And making me feel oh so full.

It stole away any thoughts and concerns about what the hell he was talking about, or how he seemed to peer into my mind. I was coming to learn that my uncle was a strange guy, but that... it made him near irresistible to me.

My legs wrapped around his ass as he bucked into me, my body pinned to the bed as I gasped for breath.

"Oh my god, just like that," I begged, my wet pussy squeezing his dick in appreciation.

And he gave it to me. Just like that.

His lean, muscular form undulated over top of me, and he began to pump his dick into me deep and hard. He was known as the fanciful artist of the family, yet he knew how to fuck. Perhaps better than any of the rest of us.

And he squeezed my breast, as he angled his hips perfectly, feeding me that hard, veiny cock with his rising thrusts.

"Mmm, you like the feel of that? You live for the feel of that incestuous, raw, virile shaft making you whole, don't you Priestess?" he grunted out.

"God, yes," I gasped, no word of a lie on my lips or in my body. He seemed to have a way of knowing things he shouldn't, and it really didn't matter in that moment. As long as I was getting what I wanted. What I needed.

My back glided against the fine, silk sheets. I clung to them, so that he could fuck me deeper, make me ache with his sexual prowess.

Uncle Arthur was to be my final conquest. My big finale. But I was finding out, I was a little outclassed by his world class charm and seduction. And I was moaning and screaming beneath him in that private manor at the edge of the estate, as he pounded me ravenously, skillfully.

"Mmph... fuck you're tight and tasty, sweet niece," he husked, as I saw his chest glisten beneath his dark hair. "And I've been away so long... so pent up with need to sew my seed," he said in his deliciously seductive husk.

My eyes rolled up in my head as the scent of our arousal filled my nostrils. I breathed out curses and whimpers of pleasure, my taut thighs pulling him in, time and time again.

His words did nothing to dissuade me, even though maybe they should have. A normal girl wouldn't find that so tempting, the idea of her uncle breeding her like a bitch in heat.

But I was a Hawthorne, and I'd quickly learned that our family was nothing close to normal.

"So do it, if you think you have such a shot at it, Uncle," I purred, leaning up to lick his neck.

His shoulders tensed up, muscles bulging as he pumped into me hard and fast. My words seeming to have some effect on him at last... or perhaps it was just coincidence in the timing.

"Mmm, I do. And I will," he growled at me, suddenly rewarding my lippy words with a hard thrust that made me scream. I would've been more able to handle it, but the fact I'd been fucking non-stop for days, made it hurt extra hard.

It was delightful, and I was happily losing my mind. My cries filled the room, my cunny walls squeezing him in reward for his harsh abuse of my precious pussy.

My nails dug into his back as my spine arched, my head pressed to the mattress as my body lost all control. I was cumming, and there was no holding back, no denying the impact that his cock had on me. It was the complete opposite to Malcolm, a total surrendering of power and the upper hand to him. To my forbidden uncle with his delicious cock and strange gifts that aren't really gifts.

And uncle Arthur pounded through my climax, that tight cunny gripping his shaft so intensely as wetness splattered his thighs and groin. He grunted and kept going, his dick swelling up and spurting some pre-cum into me as he looked down like a man frenzied with lust himself.

"I'm gonna blow," he grunted out, shivering. "I'm gonna claim your fertile little valley, sweet niece," he declared with a shudder of illicit desire.

We were long past the point of turning back, not that either of us wanted to. We both understood the path we were walking, even more so than me and any other member of my family. With them, there'd been fears, concerns, worries.

With Uncle Arthur, both of us knew that, in time, this was where we'd end up.

My pussy tightened around him, my body begging for his seed.

"Give it to me," I pleaded.

"Oh I will," he growled out in promise as his one hand squeezed my breast tightly, and he upped his game. He made me scream and cry out, as his ravenous, insatiable fucking grew harder, faster. He managed to make my body hurt in such delicious ways as he muttered filthy words under his breath until it was all gibberish to me like some alien language.

And then as I felt his dick swell, throb, he threw back his head for a loud cry, "Ye--aahhh!" He shoved his dick in deep and began to fill me with his pent up, virile seed. Such rich streams of his spunk flooded into me up as he trembled and roared with pleasure and triumph.

I clung to him with everything I had, arms and legs wrapped around him, my limbs draped in priceless finery of a princess long past. It was strange to be in such ethereal wear, but it felt meant for me, in a strange way, and in that moment, I felt like I was a Goddess.

I'd brought my entire family to their knees, made them unload in my pussy, all of them wanting a chance to breed me. To make me theirs.

I'd accomplished everything I'd set out to do. Every man I sought to charm, had trembled in climax atop me. None had been able to resist my seduction, not my brothers, not my uncle, not my father. In the end my pussy had milked each of their shafts dry, and they'd been eager for more.

So I felt a thrill and power in that moment like never before, as I lay beneath uncle Arthur, feeling him twitch and moan. I felt like nothing in the world could stop me from achieving my goals and dreams.

He seemed lost in his own thoughts, or perhaps just in the post orgasmic absence of thoughts, and I idly stroked along his spine. I enjoyed his weight atop me. It was comforting, warm, and the post coital throbs of his cock were a delight in and of themself.

I didn't want to speak, to ruin the serenity and peace that filled the room, so I just held him as our breathing slowly returned to normal.

We lay there like that a nice long while, and when finally he pulled out of me, we made out. And I saw that there were no regrets in him. We even shared some more wine, before I had to leave and tend to other affairs.

Nine

My days and nights were busy after that, with so many needy, horny men to serve around the clock. I could barely find time for anything else but fucking and taking dick. But... in all honesty, I wasn't complaining.

But once it was confirmed, and my once taut, flat tummy began to swell, so began the convincing.

Father was elated, of course. To have another child with me was at the top of his wishlist. And when I told him the news, we immediately made love in his bed, with his hands tenderly caressing my stomach. He wasn't even particularly fazed by the news that... it might've been one of my brother's kids inside me. He just said, "If this one's not mine, then the next one will be."

Malcolm took me out on his yacht, and we vanished for a couple days. He was, at first, a bit distraught that it might not be his. But he came around, and we enjoyed the days out on the water together. His dick barely went down in between nutting in me or on me.

Uncle Arthur took it all in stride, giving me a soft smile, touching my stomach a while. He had a serious look on his face then, and when he opened his eyes he said, "This one's not mine. But... maybe the next one," and kissed me deeply.

But of course Victor was the first to find out.

And I mean, really the first. I swear, I had no idea how aware of my body he was until it was him that told me I was pregnant. He couldn't even describe how he knew. He just did, and when I took the pregnancy test, that confirmed it.

"Well, fuck, I would have planned a special date, if I'd known... I was thinking it'd still be too early to find out," I said, watching his hand trail over my stomach, up between my bare breasts. I had snuck into his room that night, taking a little risk because I'd missed him so much.

"Oh, we'll make time for something special," he said with such a grin of excitement. We made love then, but I wasn't sure what he'd meant by 'something special'.

Not until the time came.

Ten

I was showing, well and obviously. My stomach was big and round and by that point, the men of the manor were carving up all my time between them. But Victor managed to sweep me away, off into the mountains, where the family had an old 'cabin'. And 'cabin' is a very loose term here, because it was an old gothic looking manor built among the trees, into the hillside. With its tall towers, it was definitely from another age, centuries old.

It was rarely used by the family anymore, because it was so out of the way, lacking some of the luxuries the rest of the family took for granted. But it had that moody look that Victor and I so loved, and it was nice and secluded.

Normally we'd have hiked part of the way, but

with my advanced pregnancy, we flew up there in the family helicopter instead.

It was really quite romantic. Victor had packed food to last us a few days, and he had it cutely packed in a picnic basket, though it was state of the art and refrigerated so that nothing would spoil on the trip. But looking at the cabin as he started leading me to it felt like being a little girl in a fairy tale.

The Hawthorne Estate was massive. Almost too massive to be awed by, because you couldn't see everything even in a day. But this place was the perfect size to catch one's breath in their chest. I'd only been there once before, and it was many years ago, back when I didn't appreciate just how beautiful it was.

"Victor," I said with a soft smile, turning to look at him. My hair was carefully braided around my crown, keeping it easier to maintain for my pregnancy, and I wore a soft, white gown that dipped low between my breasts. I wasn't ashamed of my prominent pregnancy bump, and the way Victor fawned over it, I knew he was just as fascinated by it as I.

He smiled at me, leaning down to place his lips to mine. And we kissed so sweetly on the doorstep to the country manor. Until finally he bent down and grasped me in his strong arms, and he hoisted me up, carrying me across the threshold like we were husband and wife.

The tall foyer that greeted us had been recently cleaned by the staff, who came up in anticipation of us to prepare it. But it still had that romantic gloom to it, and he brought me up to the master bedroom, before putting me down again.

"I don't get you all to myself," he said as he caressed my cheek and my pregnant belly, "but for a little while... you're all mine, right here. And I get to celebrate the baby we have on the way," he remarked, dressed so nicely in his black pants, with the sharp black jacket he had on.

"Oh Victor," I said, my arms wrapping around him. "I hope you'll be happy with me for the rest of our lives. With the path we've walked. I've never felt so alive, and it's all because of you." My grey eyes scanned his face, my heart thudding as I confessed to him. "We may not live as husband and wife, but we'll always live as soulmates."

He smiled down at me so tenderly, his strong hands moving with such delicate care as he slid the straps of my dress down from my shoulders. He calmly, quietly exposed my engorged breasts, which looked bigger, and definitely felt heavier, since the pregnancy had developed. And then he slid it down off me entirely before stripping off his own jacket and top, leaving his hard, muscular form exposed.

"Even getting to share you is a joy that I dared not imagine too long ago, sweet Prissy," he said with a smile, as he popped open the top button of his trousers.

"I dream of you, even still. Of our first tender kiss, which set my mind and body aflame. It was so forbidden, but I couldn't stop thinking about it, stop thinking about you. I thought, maybe, if I gave in, that it would help rid me of these dark, forbidden fantasies. Yet even as your child grows in me, I can't help but feel that spark. That excitement. As if this were our first time, all over again."

He worked open his pants, then pushed them down as his thick, hard cock burst out, so eager and ready. And he went to his knees before me, those strong hands caressing my thighs, my hard, pregnant belly. He caressed and worshipped every inch of me, kissing my smooth skin as he did so.

"Oh Priss... you look more beautiful than ever right now. It really is like starting all over again from the beginning," he said with an adoring smile, as one hand came up to lift a heavy breast, to caress around my nipple.

He made me feel like a Queen, and I let him

explore my skin. I'd lost some of my tan since getting pregnant, as I heard too much sun can be harmful. In fact, there was a lot I'd cut out, to give my baby its best chance. I wasn't taking any risks, but I looked into it, and I knew that fucking wasn't a risk. Not until my water broke, at least.

That was a relief to learn, because of all my vices, dick was my favourite.

"Do you really mean it? Uncle Arthur had a painting commissioned of me, but it won't be ready until after I give birth."

He kissed my stomach, then my inner thighs. And he caressed me all over as he got in between my legs, inhaling my scent.

"Mmm, I hope he puts it somewhere we can all enjoy. Because you are the finest work of art I've ever seen at this moment, sis," he said with an affectionate smile up at me, before his lips met my pussy, and he began to tongue me with such masterful care, making my clit sing as he ate me out.

I held onto his head for balance, his mouth knowing my body so well. Even as it changed through the pregnancy, he simply adjusted, found what made me cry out, where I was sensitive at that moment. He was so diligent, so loving, and my heart swelled for him. My pussy, too. It was dripping wet, eager for his mouth to devour my honey.

Getting eaten out wasn't high on my list of priorities, with how cock addicted I'd become. But it felt so nice to have his lips and tongue upon my pussy, to feel it soothing the aches of my well-pounded labia. He lavished those folds with such affection and care, and from him I experienced such blissful tingles of pleasure as his strong hands squeezed my thighs.

"Victor, I love you," I breathed out. I was always honest with him. I'd played my game with the others, but honesty was my path forward. Still, Victor was the only one I could be really truthful with, about everything. Daddy and the others didn't care too much to hear the details about each other's techniques, but Victor was always wanting to improve for me, so he wanted to know if any of them did something I liked. Even a little. Then he'd put his own spin on it, and I'd get lost to an evening of bliss.

So despite being the family cock sleeve, it was Victor who gave it to me best still. With his intimate knowledge of my body, of what I wanted. And so it was little surprise that his tongue work had me working towards a panting, gasping peak so quickly. His broad, muscular shoulders tensed up as he held me in place and ate me out with such intensely dedicated tongue movements.

My fingers tightened around his head as my body was struck with fireworks. I screamed, filling the gothic halls with my pleasured cry. My pussy throbbed against his diligent mouth, and he didn't let me squirm away, not at first. He made me take that pleasure, feel that orgasm as it rushed through me with such perfect intensity. I was so much more sensitive in my pregnancy, and he knew it, loved it, worked me up to such perfect heights before letting me crash down on his tongue.

"Fuck, fuck! Stop!" I gasped finally, releasing his head and pushing myself back, my world spinning. "Holy fuck, how are you so good at that?"

He rose up from between my legs, licking his lips and using the back of his hand to wipe some of the excess honey from around his mouth. He grinned down at me, such love and adoration in his eyes as he took hold of his shaft, then began to tease the tip of it along my sensitive, tingling folds.

"Passion drives me to improvement, sis," he said as he continued to tease me.

"God, you got me so sensitive I feel like I might cum again just from you teasing me," I moaned, my arms wrapping around his neck, tugging him onto the bed with me. "I swear, we were made for each other, brother. Nothing could have interrupted our love affair. And I think the best is yet to come, if you keep advancing your technique."

Of course, as I pulled him up over me atop the bed, he let his cock slip inside me. That thick girth stretched open my pussy, making me moan as he sank in slowly, carefully, but deeply. And he kissed my lips so lovingly, so passionately as his cock pulsated within my already pregnant depths.

"Mmm, there is so much more to come, sis... I could never grow tired of you. And all the wonders of your perfect body," he rumbled, a strong hand gently squeezing one of my tender breasts.

I felt so ready to pop, but I had another couple of months ahead of me. Still, my nervous system was working in overdrive, making every delicate touch tingle and echo through my body for intense moments of bliss.

"When we're here, in this cabin, we live as man and wife," I said, my breathy voice stern, giving him an order.

He kissed me passionately again, his hips rocking, pumping that thick cock into me slowly and carefully. He didn't want to hurt our baby, but he still made it feel good as he pumped that dick into me deeply.

"Mmm fuck, you **are** my wife... I don't care what anyone else thinks. How many other men I have to share you with, you're my wife. In our souls, we are husband and wife, Priss," he panted out to me, as his stunningly sculpted body rocked, pumping his shaft into me.

I lay back on the bed, my limbs relaxed, letting him fuck me at his own tempo, his own intensity. I didn't need to control him, or do anything to control his love making. He knew what I needed and when and how, even before I did.

It wasn't surprising that another warm flood of orgasmic pleasure began washing over me, even before he seemed to be approaching his own release. I didn't fight it back. I just let it claim me, crying out with blissful lust.

He ran his hands down to my legs, lifting them up so he could control the pace and tempo better, as well as the depth. His cock sliding in as deep as he'd dare without risking impacting our unborn child. He shivered and moaned, making my tits jiggle atop my chest as he stared down at me longingly.

"Fuck you're beautiful, sis... the bride of my dreams, and you're all mine... for a while," he panted out, his dick swelling and throbbing as he worked us both towards such a pleasurable climax. And he let one hand move up my thigh, his thumb teasing in against my clit as he bucked into me.

I was so sensitive, my head tilting from side to side as I gasped for air. He wasn't going to take it easy on me, and the tide of my last orgasm hadn't even receded before the next wave was engulfing me.

"Victor!" I screamed, not holding anything back. I didn't have to, ever again. My pussy tightened around him as honey began to drip from me.

"Prissy!" he gasped out, as his own cock was squeezed and wrung tightly by my pussy. And he was pumping into me with such desperate need to empty his loins. And as I screamed out, a flood of honey coating his shaft, his groin, he began to cum with me. Thick strands of his creamy white seed shot off, then he pulled out of me...

He grasped his dick, and milked it. Spraying more of his virile cum over my belly, splattering it upon my mons, my vulva, my thighs, even hitting my tits as he emptied his balls onto me, moaning and groaning so sensually as he did.

It wasn't like he was trying to knock me up anymore, and he was enjoying the freedom of painting me in his cum. The feeling of it landing upon my skin sent an illicit shiver through me, my own juices soaking into the bed as he left me achingly empty.

My hand went to my breast, finding the cum there, rubbing it around my hard little nipple as I rode out the end of my orgasm, panting for breath.

"Victor, I love you. I'll never tire of you."

"I could never dream of tiring of you, not even in my worst nightmares, Prissy," he assured me, as he got up on the bed beside me and bent down. We made out as I rubbed his cum into my own body, lavishing in that seed of his, enjoying the lingering feeling of how he'd marked me.

And it was a trip I would never soon forget. Most of it was too personal and precious for me to even speak aloud.

Eleven

༄

I was very nearly ready to pop, when the news came: grandfather had passed away. None of us were happy about that, even though it meant some of us--or one of us, or all of us--were about to benefit greatly. But as much as we'd played our games to earn his inheritance, we all adored and admired him.

But after the funeral, we were all summoned into one of the estate's biggest rooms, the fancy room with many chairs, sofas, divans and expensive rugs and artwork. The lawyer for the estate came in as the lot of us--Uncle Arthur, Father, Malcolm, Victor and I--sat waiting. I was the only one sitting, actually. The others were all fanned out around me, giving me encouraging touches, longing glances, or adoring smiles.

It was still a little strange, with the truth all out

there. They all coveted me for themselves in private, but they'd managed to get along very well, all together. I'd impressed upon each of them, in their own way, how important it was that we all be in this as a family. Family is very important to me, after all.

Of course, part of that arrangement meant we had to come up with some plan to share my time between them. The peace wouldn't hold if they felt I was ignoring some and favouring others. So I had to split my time up roughly evenly between them all, with certain nights scheduled to certain men. But I got to set the schedule, and... frankly I loved it. I never had to go without dick or pleasure.

And I sat there, in an elegant dress, which complimented my pregnant figure, and some high heels. It wouldn't do to show up to such an important event looking like a slob, even if I felt like I just wanted to lay in bed until the pregnancy was over.

The men all reassured me repeatedly I would be looked after well, no matter what happened. But then the lawyer began to talk.

"To Arthur, goes the guest house. It's his to keep now, along with a small share of the fortune," said the lawyer after the boring preamble. And uncle Arthur looked unsurprised.

"Next, to Malcolm goes the fleet of yachts, and the

marina. As well as the island resort," and Malcolm brimmed excitedly at that. He leaned over and whispered to me.

"We'll have so many good times there, Prissy," he squeezed my thigh and grinned.

"To my eldest son, I leave control of the company and his generous salary. As well as the family's private jet," and Father looked a bit disappointed but not surprised. He earned a lot heading up the family's operations, so receiving nothing beyond that didn't really hurt him.

"To Victor, I leave the family cabin up in the mountains. As well as the helicopter. And a sizeable stipend from the estate, totalling a hundred million dollars," said the lawyer, and Victor looked pleased, grinning at me.

"It's our little private getaway. And we're set for life," Victor said with a grin to me.

But that still left billions in assets, not the least of which was the estate.

"And finally, to my dearest Priscilla... you were always the sweetest of the family. The best of us all. And the only one pushing forward with the next generation of Hawthornes. So to you I leave the rest of the family fortune, and the estate. May you use your inheritance to bring peace and prosperity to this family," and the lawyer rattled off the list of assets that included. From the billions of dollars worth of shares and investments, to the cars, the property and... oh God I lost track!

Everyone was a little stunned, and we sat in silence. Except for Victor who took my hand, squeezed it, and kissed the back of it.

"You deserve this," Victor said with a smile, and soon the rest of the family were following suit.

But the lawyer interjected soon thereafter.

"He also left a letter, just for you, Priscilla," said the lawyer, getting up and handing me the wax sealed envelope. "I don't know what's in it. But... it's all yours. He asks that you read it in private, and share the contents with nobody," he said.

And for that reason, I can't tell you the discovery I made within that letter that made me cry. Oh, there were such sweet words. He reiterated his request for me to keep bringing peace to the family. To rein in the men of the Hawthorne line. But he also included personal stories, instructions. Reminiscences about our own sweet times together.

But the important thing is, that in the end: the future was in our hands. And most of all... my hands.

It shouldn't come as a surprise to anyone that after my first son, there were many more. As they grew older, each of them did seem to take after a different member of the family. Four sons in all, and a daughter was my most recent. Each have two years between them, and are loved beyond reason. After all, they have an entire family to take care of them and protect them forever.

As a girl adopted into this family, it was more than I could dream of. But in the end, family is always what you make of it.

Subscribe for more:
http://candyquinn.com/newsletter

Recommended For You

For a full list of all my books, or to browse by length or kink, please visit my website!

https://candyquinn.com/books

YOUR NEXT HOT READ

Taboo Passions Layla & Landon

Shipwrecked Brat

Stranded Beauty

Free Exclusive Story

LUST LESSONS: BELLA

She has the hots for teacher

Mr. Wright is totally off limits. Not only is he her teacher, but he's also her brother's best friend.

Bella has never wanted anyone more. At first, she just wants to tease him. She doesn't wear panties, and practically begs him for the big D —- detention — just to prove to him how good she is at being bad. But he wants more than a tease. He wants to claim her fertile, innocent body, and neither of them can resist their forbidden desires.

TEASER

By the time the bell rang and the other students rushed out, Bella's fantasies had her wound up tighter than a knot. Her bare pussy was dripping on her chair, and she slipped out of it eagerly.

"Well, Mr. Wright, you got me alone," she grinned.

Clark gave her a cautionary look, before he went to the door and shut it tight then locked it.

"You really chose an... interesting way to get yourself in trouble, Bella," he said to her as he returned from the door, shaking his head at her in surprised disbelief, a soft chuckle escaping his lips. "But you always were a little terror of a tease," he said as he made his way back towards the class windows, beginning to slide the curtains shut.

"You make it sound so sweet," she giggled, sitting on his desk. She pulled her white skirt out from under her, crossing her legs as she watched him shut the curtains. "I just did what felt natural."

Get your free copy of Lust Lessons: Bella, and so much more! All you have to do is subscribe to my newsletter. http://candyquinn.com/newsletter

Become Candy Obsessed

For over a decade, I've been writing the hottest, naughtiest stories I can think of, and I'm addicted. I love to explore the forbidden, the taboo, and the over-the-top sexy. Each story starts off with a sizzle, giving you that nice build up, and that perfect release.

Discover new, secret fantasies, or just indulge in those sticky-sweet guilty pleasures. I'll never judge! Make sure to follow me on your fave site so you never miss a new release.

Plus, if you sign up for my mailing list, you'll get updates on my new books, bundles, giveaways **and** a **Free, exclusive** novella.

CONNECT WITH CANDY!

candyquinn.com

candyquinn.com/newsletter

candy.quinn.erotica@gmail.com

FOLLOW ME EVERYWHERE!

Also by Candy Quinn

NOVELS

Stranded Princess

Seducing the Hawthornes

NOVELLAS

Taboo Passions Layla & Landon

Shipwrecked Brat

Stranded Beauty

Innocent Farm Girl

Precious Pet

The Fugitive

Dirty Country Love

Sylvia & Zach Collection

Protector

Mandy Collection

Nympho Farm Girl

Biker's Sugar Babe Nympho Pet

His Girl

Innocent Tease

THE DELANEY BROTHERS

Alastair

Jack

Tristan

William

TABOO STEP-DADDY

HIS BRAT'S FERTILE FIRST TIME

Avril

Blaire

Cassidy

Delilah

Raina

Taboo Temptress

Taking the Fertile Brat

The Billionaire and the Brat

Teaching the Brat

The Priest's Brat

Pregnant Brat for Christmas

Cam Girl for the Man of the House

Bratty Chrissy

Honey Trapping the Man of the House

Seducing the Man of the House

Spoiled Brat

Rich Brat

Summer Heat

Flirting with the Man of the House

Her Forbidden Cherry

Love Spell

TABOO STEP-BROTHER/SISTER

Taboo Passions Layla & Landon

Stepbrother's Baby

Valley Girl Tease

Unleashed Fantasies

Taboo Passions Lilly & Leo 1

Taboo Passions Lilly & Leo 2

Taboo Passions Lilly & Leo 3

TABOO STEP-DADDY & STEP-BROTHER MFM

TEACHER / STUDENT

AGE GAP

Buying Her Innocence

The Fertile Foreign Exchange

His Muse: Kiara

His Muse: Layla

His Muse: Stella

VIRGIN BREEDING

Hot Girl Next Door

Spoiled Matilda

Little Brat Peeps On: Fiona's First Time

Fertile First Time Tourist

Fertile First Time with a Bad Boy Biker

Fertile Model: Lights_On_Lydia

Off Limits: Rory

Fertile Bookworm

Making Sweet Music

Halloween Candy: The Costume Party

Halloween Candy: The Haunted Maze

Halloween Candy: The Scary Movie

Missed Connections: Her Hero

Missed Connections: Hometown Honey

BDSM

Nympho

Nympho Halloween

Nympho Angel

Nympho Off the Pill

Nympho for the Gang

Nympho Valentine

GANGBANG

Fertile First Time with the Team

Fertile Cheerleader

Fertile Sorority

Fertile Birthday

Fertile Freshman for the Team

SUGAR DADDIES

Sugar Baby Paige

Christine's Sugar Daddies

Karen's Sugar Daddy

Olivia's Sugar Daddy

Sugar Daddy Rock Star

Sugar Daddy Camgirl

Becca, Katie & Lynn

Fertile First Time Becca

Fertile First Time Katie

Fertile First Time Lynn

Sharing Her

Buying Her

Catering to Her

Exhibitionist for Her

Teaching Her

Rocking Her

Trading for Her

Stealing Her

Awakening Her

Punishing Her

Blindfolding Her

BUNDLES

Forbidden Temptations

Fertile Farmgirl Collection

Fertile Farms

First Taste of Candy

Taboo Brats

Tasting Candy

First Times

Candy Quinn's Dirty Fantasies

Lickable Candy Bundle

Sharing Her Bundle

Three Fertile First Times

Fertile First Time with the Gang

HARDCORE

Taboo Nympho

First Time Nympho

Punished Nympho

Bratty Nympho

Princess Nympho

Sleepy Nympho

Lustful Nympho

Ganged Nympho

Spitroasted Nympho

Spoiled Nympho

Cheating Nympho